THE KING OF A VACANT CITY

THE KING OF A VACANT CITY

SIMON LENNON

Pine Hill Books

The King of a Vacant City

Fiction

Published by Pine Hill Books

ISBN 978-1-925446-22-7 (electronic)

ISBN 978-1-925446-23-4 (paperback)

56,000 words

Cover image: The National Film and Sound Archive, 2012

To my eldest son

PREFACE

During my time working at a mining company, I'd walk from North Sydney railway station across the Pacific Highway to the office. I walked there every morning, aside from those few days in school holidays my wife didn't want our car and I drove to work. The highway was normally awash with rushing cars and pedestrians looking for breaks in the traffic, rather than waiting for green crossing lights.

One morning, there were no cars or other pedestrians. In that place that ought to have been crowded, there was only I.

A moment later, a car or person appeared. Soon it was melodic mayhem again, but that thought of sudden solitude remained with me as I walked along busy Walker Street to the office. I imagined a man waking one morning in the midst of his professional career, to see everyone else had gone.

MONDAY

Monday would be the last afternoon in which Edmund Neale longed to be left alone. Yet, more often than not, he already was.

Edmund sat engrossed to his office desk, in another of his suits and cotton shirts with pressed long sleeves and cuffs. People would've said he was handsome, as business uniforms conjured handsomeness in any man who wore them; the clothes his job required became more expensive as he progressed through his career. His clean-shaven cheeks were sharp and lean, his brown hair kept short enough to allow air behind his ears and past his collar. The first lines of what might be his age, thirty-four, slipped from the corners of his eyes. Edmund often rubbed his fingers over them trying to massage back their youthfulness. He hadn't done enough to be so old so soon.

Office furnishings were clean and functional, modest without unnecessary trimmings. Managers wanted companies to appear profitable but not so profitable as to be rich at the customers' expense or, worse still, complacent. Hired pots of green tree plants with polished leaves but no petals or pollen adorned some offices and reception areas. The calming colours of the offices, without marks or imperfections, were those that management consultants determined were the most conducive to people working.

Edmund's fashionable black leather shoes pressed against the carpet floor he couldn't see. Startling him from his concentration, his office door burst open. "When will it be ready?" boomed the chairman of directors. His face tanned from more leisure in the sun than Edmund knew, Hugh Garrett was a portly man with a thick moustache: something more to frighten people.

Edmund was drafting the company's submission to a government authority. "I should finish it tomorrow morning, Mister Garrett."

"We expect it this evening."

The time was already five o'clock. "I didn't know."

"You should've known."

"My girlfriend has tickets to a concert at the conservatorium tonight."

"You better get cracking."

Edmund contemplated saying something more, before acquiescing. Nothing ever changed for what he said.

"Sacrifice breeds success, Edmund," proclaimed the chairman, in another of his phrases. Edmund needed to work hard whether he already was successful or was still trying to succeed. "We all make sacrifices."

"Understood."

"I'm going out for a time," said Garrett, almost certainly headed to corporate hospitality or another secret meeting, befitting his perception of executive status. "You call me after seven thirty if you need anything."

The concert began at eight o'clock. "Understood."

"Good," said Garrett, clicking his fingers twice in rapid, brash succession, hurrying Edmund back to work as he might call a steward. He pulled shut the door as he departed.

Edmund at his desk tried to finish his long chore, between the interruptions of the telephone and colleagues pushing his door open to ask or tell him something. If they didn't close the door when they departed, Edmund closed it.

Hanging from the corridor and meeting room walls were large framed photographs of company businesses. Low partitions separated the secretarial and clerical desks from the corridors and each other, where people who were willing to encroach upon a line between their working and other lives discreetly affixed photographs of their loved and loving ones. Glass walls sealed the few individual offices.

At around about five thirty, the figure approaching Edmund beyond the thickened glass wasn't a colleague. Candice was dressed for work in a full blouse and skirt, but smiled for after-work. Her red lips enhanced her rounded, pretty face and glistening blonde hair, although she was more beautiful than she realised without needing to do anything about it. That natural, unearned beauty might first have drawn Edmund to her; too many people strove to make themselves less attractive than otherwise they were. Edmund stood up from his desk.

Candice opened Edmund's office door without needing to knock. In her hand was a plastic shopping bag she gave him. "I bought you this to wear tonight," she told him. "You don't want to look like you've come from the office."

Taking the bag, because he should, Edmund opened it. Inside was a striped blue shirt. "Garrett insists I finish this submission tonight and it still isn't good enough," he told her. "I don't know if can make it to the concert."

"You promised me you'd come, Edmund; you've done this to me again. Instead of doing something special, I end up alone while you make love to your career."

"Can someone else go with you?"

"Not this late, and before you ask again: No, I won't go alone. I'm not going to sit with my hair made up and in my best evening dress among a thousand happy people and an empty seat beside me."

"I'm sorry, honey."

"You're always sorry, Edmund." She grabbed the bag back from him and started to turn away. Edmund reached forward and grabbed his office door before she could close it on him. She turned back to face him. "My father gave us these tickets because he thought you'd enjoy the Bach concertos, not so I'd have a ticket for my handbag."

"I'll pay for everything, Candice: the tickets, the shirt."

"It isn't the money or the concert," she said, thrusting the bag back at him. "I work too, but I find time to see you. I'd rather be with you than without you."

"I don't do anything I don't have to do, but I have so much to do."

"Why burrow in your office if it's not to do what you want to do? You don't have to make money you don't have time to spend. You could come to the concert, finish your work in the morning, and Hugh Garrett will have to live with it."

"Would you have me lose my job?"

"You can find another one."

"This is all I can do," Edmund confessed, dissatisfied with the blandness of his reply. The door was becoming sore in his hand and he let go of it. His other hand lowered the shopping bag to his side.

Candice sighed. "Your success imprisons you as much as failure would've condemned a lesser man."

Worse than her anger, was her disappointment. "I can see you for breakfast," he told her.

"I'm having breakfast with friends. I thought we'd talk about the concert. We might talk about you."

"I can see you tomorrow night," persisted Edmund, moving towards her. She pulled away. "I'll buy you dinner at Descartes'." The restaurant was close to the building in which he worked and was the easy expensive place in which Candice liked to eat, with chef's specials every day and petit fours afterwards.

"Will I get a table by the window so I can wave up to you at your desk?"

Her words would not distract him. "I'll see you there at seven."

"I'm not sure," said Candice, the tone in her voice too serious. "The only meal I can be sure you'll eat is in your office."

"I can't do whatever I want to do," said Edmund, looking around his office box. "I'll call you in about an hour to tell you if I can make the concert."

"Call me to say you're coming. Don't call me to say you're sorry you're not." She left, striding back along the office corridor and away.

Edmund watched her leave. When she'd gone from sight, he left her shopping bag and shirt on the floor behind his desk.

Beside it was his black leather satchel, in which he carried work papers. Edmund also carried a colourful brochure for holidays to Fiji upon which he often mused aboard the train, picturing long-legged Candice in swimwear on the sand. Unable to commit to dates away from work to go there with her, he'd been carrying the brochure in his satchel for two months.

Early evening became a late autumn night outside. The telephones ringing on other people's desks became infrequent, as did the electronic mail messages appearing on his computer monitor dominating Edmund's desk. The colleagues who'd sporadically diverted him from his work throughout the day and those who hadn't, sitting at their desks and meandering about the corridors, progressively left their offices at the end of their working hours. The offices around him didn't feel as empty as they were.

A building cleaner in his checked flannelette shirt and un-ironed trousers emptied the wastepaper basket beside Edmund's feet while Edmund persevered, trying to ignore him. After vacuum cleaning the grey carpet floors of other offices, rooms, and corridors, the cleaner knocked on Edmund's office door of and looked at him through the glass wall, Edmund shook his head to send him away.

Soon after seven o'clock, Edmund remained far from finishing. He conducted most telephone conversations from his office using the base-set microphone and speaker, which left his hands free to type or turn paper pages, but Candice objected whenever the sounds through her telephone earpiece echoed to the hollow tones of open speakers. For her, and to save himself from her consternation, he held the telephone in his hand, while his eyes perused the computer screen and working words he'd drafted. "I am sorry," he told her.

"You don't need a girlfriend," she told him. "You need a studio portrait photograph to adorn your desk and seldom pause to notice."

"I'll call you tomorrow."

"You can try." She hung up the telephone.

Without reason anymore to rush his work, Edmund took a pen and scribbled a line through the note in his desk diary about the concert. He slowly turned the page back to the previous week's entries: pending chores to complete and records of telephone conversations. The empty page for Saturday reminded him they'd eaten dinner together then. Turning another page back, the last entry for Thursday night had been a performance of *The Cherry Orchard*, with a line struck through it. If their relationship had ceased meaning anything to Candice, then the best record of their time together was Edmund's diary.

For thirteen years, he'd expended every working day and more days and nights among small offices in big buildings in one city or another, where thick multiple-glazed windows kept outside all senses of other worlds. Within the hazes of grey, the city skyline of building blocks and reaching shapes once seemed such a carousel, with brightly painted unicorns reflected in glass mirrors and peppy melodies playing without words, but years had passed since Edmund last felt very much for them: those stone, steel, and concrete structures crafted from kits of industrial design. He hadn't awaited anything or dreaded anything, aspiring only for the intermittent tasks of interest to him. No longer referring to his career as being ambition, he undertook the pattern of his weeks, his conversations across meetings and his documents and correspondence. The carousel had become a treadmill in black rubber, moving much too fast for Edmund to step away. He could only leave by jumping off, but he mightn't be able to jump back on again. He didn't know where he would be without it.

Edmund under lights sat confined to his corporate desk. Sitting there, where nobody could see him, he wasn't handsome. When his neck became sore, he loosened the tie around his collar. He stretched his back and legs from his chair. Long white fluorescent lights from the ceilings flickered too rapidly for people sitting under them to notice.

The company maintained stocks of transient, tasteless meals that people working evenings, holidays, and weekends didn't need to pause to savour. Not bothered to use the kitchen oven,

Edmund poured boiling water into a cup of beef soup packet mix.

His mind wandered to Candice and the concert, before he dragged his concentration back to the company objective. He didn't have the time to let her distract his tired attention. Time was always pressing and all the participants at a seminar Edmund attended received clocks like the small grey one atop the filing cabinets facing his long desk.

Hanging nonchalantly from frames that filled his office wall were Edmund's aging university degrees. More than a mirror of his past, the menagerie of scrolled italics under glass had been a ticket to a future not yet cast upon him, but his corporate title and professional accreditations only mattered because they lay printed with his name on matte-paper business cards.

Office telephones rarely rang at night, letting people concentrate upon their work, but Edmund answered his telephone before his recorded voice had the chance to reply. "Neale," he said, utilising the microphone and speaker.

"Where's the submission?" boomed the chairman's voice.

"It should be ready within the hour, Mister Garrett."

"What have you been doing?"

Edmund's fingers close to the telephone flicked the chairman's intrusive, insulting voice. They were Edmund's secret insolence, the private revolution in his mind, relieving a little of his frustration without incurring aggravation; Edmund would've known if the company operated surveillance cameras in the offices. "Preparing it," he replied, his words not drawn to reflect his thoughts. "I won't leave the office until I've finished."

"Good," replied Garrett, without sentiment. "Tomorrow I want you working on that joint venture proposal. You do that well and the directors will notice you."

Edmund replied with no more sincerity than had been conferred on him. "Thank you, Mister Garrett." The directors never noticed the work that Edmund did, unless they didn't like it.

The connection ended and Edmund resumed working, cloaked in a cogent anarchy of papers and materials. They fed his fractured mind with arguments and intuition, while he drank mugs of lukewarm coffee as he'd drunk them through the day. Littered by the keyboard were little metal clips that once held paper sheets together, which his impatiently idle fingers twisted from their manufactured form into random, useless shapes. His distant abstract brain struggled with a problem and a pressure until it reached an incremental resolution, when those fingers vented their energy typing letters on the keyboard.

The submission that had been almost interesting to Edmund early in its unfolding argument became more gruelling with every revision. Words that once flowed through the computer screen ground against his weary eyes. The facts and inferences from them that he inscribed were those that he already knew and that some people believed. He rubbed his hands through his hair and over the skin around his eyes, massaging his muscles to stay awake. He glanced at the time in the corner of his computer screen and wondered why he did.

Long after midnight, much too late to see Candice at her home, Edmund finished. He transmitted the draft submission to the directors' computers and filed the papers he wouldn't need to read again too soon back in the cabinets of his office. The papers he might soon need to check he placed back into neat piles along the front of his desktop, beside the piles of papers of his next most pressing projects and a larger pile of clear plastic sleeves containing papers of lesser chores. His printed copy of the submission consoled him his chore was complete, until somebody instructed him to change it.

Loose pens and blank sheets of paper he returned to the top drawer beside his chair. Bent paper clips he swept into his hand and into the rubbish bin on the floor. Most of the pale desk surface was clean when first he saw it every morning and clean again at the end of every day; menial tasks helped his mind slow down from working.

His jacket had been hanging from the hook behind his office door for more than fifteen hours when he dressed back into it, checking his wallet was still in the inside pocket. He took his mobile telephone from the shelves behind his desk, hoping not to hear a telephone ring again that night. The cleaners had long left the floor and gone to wherever cleaners went. The odours of cleaning fluids had dissipated leaving the building without any defining smells. Nothing in the offices ever smelt.

Carrying his satchel on his shoulder and Candice's shopping bag in his hand, Edmund ran his tired fingers over the panel of black plastic switches by the door from the reception area, extinguishing the ceiling lights above him, around the reception desk, and throughout the empty premises. His keys locked shut the doors; the security card he needed to enter the building and offices out of working hours wasn't necessary to leave them. Someone coming to the office in the morning earlier than he arrived would reopen them.

"Ground floor," said the computer voice made to sound like a woman's voice, speaking from a panel in the lift. It excused him from the building.

More cars than usual moved along the city street so late at night, but Edmund was too sleepy to think about them. The only pedestrians were a uniformed policewoman gently leading by the hand a homeless man, wearing a blanket for a coat above his refuse clothes and holding a polystyrene cup. It reminded Edmund why he worked so hard.

Waiting at the rank that night, shining under street lights, was a single peculiarly white taxi. Through the windscreen, the elderly driver watched Edmund approach. Traveling alone, Edmund normally sat in the front seats of taxicabs. That night, he had no mood to listen to conversations that taxi drivers made. He opened a rear door.

"Have you heard the news?" the driver asked him.

"Just take me home," said Edmund, closing the door beside him and telling the driver his home address.

"Don't you..."

"Please," Edmund interrupted, offering him a token courtesy more than he felt like giving. "I've too much on my mind."

The driver studied him for a moment, before nodding. "You want time alone." Facing Edmund, a crucifix hung from the driver's rear-vision mirror.

Edmund turned his head towards the policewoman helping the homeless man into her police car, while the taxi pulled away from the kerb. Harsh lines of lights rolled past the windows, while Edmund sat in the back seat with his arm across his satchel and shopping bag resting against his thigh. Rising thoughts of Candice threatening to end their relationship before it had ever gone too far competed with receding thoughts about the submission he'd surrendered the day and night to make, without distracting him from noticing where the taxi went. "This is not the quickest route," said Edmund.

"I thought we could avoid the worst of the traffic," the driver replied, watching the street ahead of him.

"It's the middle of the night."

The traffic was busier than Edmund was used to seeing so late at night, but he dared not remark upon it. In the absence of anything more, the only measure of his success had become the perceptions made by people he'd never before seen and never saw again. Success was simply keeping what he had.

"Up here on the right," said Edmund, guiding the driver to the kerb outside the apartment building in which he lived, much like those around. He checked the meter display as the driver told him the fare, contemplating paying less than that amount because of the route the driver took. He would not waste his time in a dispute.

"Thank you," said the driver, accepting Edmund's company credit card. He processed the fare and charge before Edmund entered his security number into the credit card terminal. "You get what you need when you ask the right person," the driver told him, "although it mightn't be what you think you want."

"My card," said Edmund.

The driver returned Edmund's credit card to him. "Good night."

"Not so far."

The taxi driver laughed. "Be wary of what you want, Mister Neale. You might get it."

Everything in his apartment was neatly in its place, until Edmund dumped his satchel and shopping bag on the lounge room floor. The answering machine for his fixed-line telephone hadn't recorded any messages, as he'd pretty well expected. (Sometimes he wondered why he bothered keeping a home telephone.) He disengaged the machine so it wouldn't start to play before he reached the telephone, as Edmund normally did when he returned home.

Something thumped a window and Edmund turned around; the only open window in his apartment was a small one high in the bathroom. A bird must have struck the glass, although birds didn't normally fly at night.

He hung his jacket and trousers on a coat hanger in his bedroom cupboard and dropped his shirt, socks, and underclothes in the washing machine in the small laundry beyond the kitchen alcove, to clean next weekend. Dressed into his lazy grey tracksuit too tired to brush his teeth, he crashed into his double bed for one. His soft pillow held his head, while his crumpled sheets enveloped him.

He'd not switched on the television set or radio. They wouldn't have taught him anything anyway.

2

TUESDAY MORNING

His clock radio shook Edmund from his sleep too early Tuesday, as it shook him too early every weekday. In the small light of dawn, his eyes flexed and found their gaze in the blank space of the cream white walls and ceiling of his bedroom. The sounds from his bedside radio slowly crystallised into music his brain almost recognised, while his body remained rigid in his sleep. His breath gradually became full breathing, clearing away the night, progressively reviving his senses for the day. He yawned; the day not yet started already tired him.

Strength rose slowly back inside his chest and limbs. Becoming lucid, Edmund reluctantly dragged himself from bed, beginning the process taking him to his office.

The bathroom mirror reflected his ruffled hair and eyes sleeping part way in their lids. The first tap water was always cold, until he adjusted the hot stream to make it bearable. The soft buzzing of the electric razor ebbed with the contours of his cheeks and chin, carefully capturing every whisker from another day alive. "Don't ever wear a beard, Edmund," Hugh Garrett once advised him. "Men with beards hide the truth like they hide their faces."

Within the closed door to the shower recess, hot water under pressure pounded over him, washing his flesh and hair. Stepping out, his warm skin quickly cooled, water dripping to the floor. A blue towel doused his body dry, before he wrapped it around his waist. Nobody wanted to appear as if he or she perspired, and Edmund sprayed unscented deodorant under his arms.

Dressed into another sharp and clean white shirt, the crimson-patterned tie and suit he picked weren't those he'd worn yesterday. Edmund wore the fabrics and cuts of fabric, numbers of buttons, and shapes of pockets according to the objectively ordained fashions of the offices: silver-grey suits in summer, charcoal grey and deep blue suits in winter, which made any man seem taller than he did without them. Edmund cast them aside when new fashions dictated he stop wearing them.

He fastened his watch band to his left wrist, forced his feet into his shoes, and switched off the radio. A glass tumbler filled with refrigerated orange juice concluded his routine, invigorating his stomach back to work.

With Edmund's remote control handset, the television set came to life, but only static played across the screen and from the speakers around the lounge room. He changed the channel, but could only get static on every channel. "Damn," he said, annoyed that something so expensive was malfunctioning, switching off the set.

A Friday morning maid kept his apartment free from marks and dust, but Edmund checked the tumbler base hadn't left a damp ring on the glass-topped coffee table. If he sat in the deep cushions of his restful sofa or an armchair, then standing up again would be too difficult. Lemon marmalade on slices of toasted bread again sweetened his lips and mouth, while he imagined Candice eating croissants and cappuccino coffee in a cafeteria, her blonde hair sparkling in the sunrise, complaining to her friends about him and telling them whether she would meet him that evening. Edmund placed his soiled glassware and crockery in the kitchen dishwasher.

He stashed his wallet in a pocket inside his jacket and collected his case of keys and security cards. The wall mirror inside the door helped him brush his hair before anyone but he could see it. Sunglasses across his eyes and his satchel hanging from his shoulder, Edmund left his apartment, locking the door behind him.

The lift doors opened soon after Edmund pressed the button in the wall beside them. He stepped forward into the empty lift, pressed the button for the ground floor of the building, and watched the doors close in front of him. The sounds of falling and rising weights commenced, while the lift too slowly descended and thoughts of the day ahead filtered through his mind. Hugh Garrett and other directors might spend days considering his submission without sharing their thoughts with him, or they might berate him when he arrived at the office for what he'd done or hadn't done. He would accede to their inconsequential nuances and might debate their deeper points with them, be right but not convince them. They could then claim his work as being their own if it succeeded and dispel blame to him for failure.

Edmund dared not let the chores he needed to commence or complete that day delay his arrival at Descartes' restaurant, if Candice was going to be there. He would telephone her confirming their rendezvous, in response to which her words explicit or oblique would tell him whether their relationship survived the thoughts he suffered.

Opening the timber door from the building foyer, the cool air chilled Edmund's face and hands. Stepping outside, he stopped, without walking down the few stairs to the footpath. The city street before him, which normally bustled with pedestrians and moving cars, was empty, without people anywhere.

Removing his sunglasses to see everything more clearly, Edmund looked around. He'd never before seen the street so vividly devoid of people. The only cars were the few parked at kerbs where dozens were parked yesterday. The time was nearing eight o'clock: not too early or too late.

No men or women in business suits or casual wear strode along the footpaths along which they strode every other morning, walking to their work or leisure. The streets that ordinarily were loud lay silent: empty of everyone but Edmund, standing alone atop the stairs.

A sudden storm might close everything, but the sky was clear and blue. The air was dry. Nobody else stood at apartment building doors or windows, wondering where all the people were. Nothing moved.

Tuesday might've been a public holiday about which Edmund had forgotten; fewer people and cars traversed the streets around his home on weekends and public holidays than did on working days. He checked the date in his mind. Public holidays weren't usually on Tuesdays, and Monday had been a normal working day, with talk of things to do and people to see on Tuesday.

The day might've been an extraordinary public holiday commemorating something good; he could telephone Candice to invite her to see him sooner than seven o'clock that evening. Perhaps a great sporting victory overnight had prompted a sudden holiday, but no major sporting events had been held that evening past. He chastised himself for doubting what he knew to be true; the day was one for working among the endless litany of working weeks and years.

Edmund would see cars and people soon enough; he mightn't have noticed the lack of people other days. He replaced his sunglasses to his face, adjusted his satchel on his shoulder, and proceeded down the steps.

Walking along the footpath, paved from kerb to building, through the fresh air towards the railway station, Edmund appreciated no one standing in his way to slow his pace. Nobody hurried past him, forcing him to change his step. The silence of the streets amplified the sounds he'd never before heard: his eerie feet tapping against the footpath; his sleeves brushing against his jacket. He couldn't hear any human being but him.

The footpath opened into a cross-street intersection. Edmund slowed, looking up and down the roadways in each direction abating into blocks of shops, offices, and more apartment buildings. On the footpath without company, he stopped walking.

Without the sound of him moving, everything was quiet: no sound of anything. Traffic lights shone as if cars would imminently require them. None did. The lights were something ordinary, when little else that morning was. Electric lights shone from some shops and the entrances to some buildings, the doors of which were closed. The building corner where somebody sold flowers some mornings or early evenings was empty. Nobody came towards or walked away from him.

In the centre of the footpath lay a child's teddy bear. Edmund picked it up, as if that might move its owner to cry out. It didn't. Edmund left the bear beside the nearest apartment building steps.

Near him was a grocery store, where a portly shopkeeper and his wife in red-and-white-striped aprons laughed about their children's antics. Public holidays that closed other eateries had never closed that store, but it too was closed, without a notice to explain. In that day of the empty city, Edmund knew that it would be.

He might've been asleep, but the visions through his eyes were clear. He felt his arms and legs; he was awake.

The green lights shone at the pedestrian crossing before him. Edmund crossed the street. In another moment of uncertainty, he wondered if he'd slept through several days until he woke on Sunday morning when fewest people would be out. Nobody slept so long, and Hugh Garrett wouldn't let him lie so long in bed. The day was Tuesday and people walking and driving to work ought to have crowded the streets around him, as they did yesterday.

None of the shops along the footpath displayed notices of a holiday or other reason why the streets would be serene; nothing suggested the day was for anything but working. The gymnasium opened early every morning for its members and guests suffering their exertion, pumping adrenalin through their brains to hone their bodies and like themselves; he'd done the same before his work consumed him. The premises were dark. Edmund pushed at the door to confirm that it was locked; he'd thought the gymnasium was open on public holidays but could've been mistaken.

Somebody ought to have been at the brasserie: drinking varieties of teas and eating pastries. The chairs and tables remained locked inside the building; the footpath was bland without them.

Banks always notified people of days they would be closed, but no notice was affixed to the street-front windows of the branch. Nobody stood at the automatic teller machine taking money it offered to dispense.

Lights shone from a public laundry across the street, without murmurs of a life. The wall of washing machines that cleaned the clothes of solitary people waiting late at night was still.

Sometimes Edmund walked slowly, watching everything around him, expecting to see somebody in every coming minute. Sometimes he walked quickly to bring him to that person sooner; the day would then cease being curious.

Through the windows of a delicatessen, Edmund thought he saw movement. He hurried towards it, but could not see anyone through the glass. The door was locked, but he knocked loudly, calling out "Are you open?" No one answered.

Across the street, the entranceway to the railway station, normally crowded with people hurrying to catch a train, was empty. The tiny newsagent normally selling newspapers and magazines was closed. The bistro normally serving short breakfasts and faster food was dark.

Edmund strode across the street without waiting for the pedestrian lights to change; a policeman's reprimand would've been to his relief. He entered the station concourse, where the sprawling floor reflected the electric lights shining brightly from the ceiling. Removing his sunglasses from his eyes, he went to a ticket-vending booth to ask an attendant to tell him about the holiday that day. The booth was closed.

A second booth was also closed. Machines had made people unnecessary. Nobody stood at the machines.

The turnstiles through the barricades to the platforms were closed, without station staff ensuring that people didn't climb over them, as they might not on public holidays. Beside them, with a ticket sensor too, a metal gate was open. Edmund walked past the lax surveillance, which couldn't know he carried a travel card in his wallet. The nearest of the still escalators started to move downward as Edmund approached, activating sensors in the floor.

Alighting from the moving stairs, the long platform was stark and empty, as it would be after a train departed before the next pending passengers arrived. Emptiness that morning no longer surprised him. Edmund rarely boarded a train on weekends and public holidays, when he drove his car to his office or anywhere else. The confines of the platform might be so desolate on a sudden public holiday.

Slowly, the sound and vibrations of a train coming rumbled through the ground and soles of his shoes. Edmund relaxed, folding his sunglasses with the fingers of one hand, stowing them in the top pocket of his jacket. The train appeared on the track, its lights shining and carriages bustling, coming towards him, away from the city centre.

It didn't slow. The driver at the window must have seen him, but didn't slow. Instead, the train sped past him. Through the carriage windows, Edmund watched standing and seated silhouettes rushing past him through the station; passengers were normally fewer in number on public holidays, except for the most special days. The train's rear shrank as it turned and disappeared away. The vibrations through his feet soon abated.

Overhead monitors that normally displayed the destinations of coming trains and the times before which they would arrive were blank. They might've been malfunctioning or the stationmaster mightn't have had anything to report. An industrial dispute might be affecting services or the station's operation.

The time on the old, round clock near the monitors was that on Edmund's watch: eight fifteen. The escalators behind him stopped. The station was again silent, but for the sounds that Edmund made.

The day and date displayed in his mobile telephone were those of Tuesday, an ordinary day. Through his telephone, Edmund checked the railway timetable. Two services should've passed through the station in the time he'd stood there, if that was a working weekday. One service was soon coming, if the day was a public holiday. Train services were normally less frequent on public holidays and weekends than they were on working days.

The time on the platform clock and on his watch moved

slowly forward, towards the time he was due at work. Cursing the unreliability of railway services, Edmund walked to the front edge of the platform, from which he looked up the track towards the train to soon arrive, longing for the trackside signal lights to change. He stood alone in silence, where normally he stood among a crowd with noise. Some people read, if only the posters along the walls they'd already read. Candice had seen the film *Millstone Vanquished* with her friends at a cinema while he was working at his office, although he'd been less interested than she'd been in a film about a hummingbird in an acorn farm. Edmund was normally among the morning clamour; the air remained cold without it.

He slipped money into a vending machine, pressed the button for coffee without milk or sugar, and heard the sounds of a mechanism releasing a paper cup. Looking down at the serving tray, no cup appeared, but hot water poured from the spout. "Damn," he said aloud, cursing his misfortune.

Again pressing the button before pounding his hand on the machine, the water splashed a little and drained away. Another sound ought to have dropped a serving of bad, ground coffee beans, but only their meek aroma hinted at the taste he might've had.

Edmund checked the machine to see if his money had been refunded. "Damn." A notice specified the telephone number he should call to report faults in the machine or exhausted supplies.

The signal lights that changed when trains approached didn't change. No train came along the track. Nor did any train come to the other side of the platform. The escalators remained still and nobody walked onto the platform. The speakers from which announcements of late-running trains came were quiet.

Edmund again drew his mobile telephone from his pocket and dialled the number for the offices at which he worked. "This office is presently unattended," said the message Hugh Garrett's personal assistant long ago recorded. "If you know the extension of the person to whom you want to speak, you may dial that number at any time. If you would like to leave a message, then please do so after the tone. We will attend to you when possible."

The tone sounded. "June, it's Edmund. The trains are running late. I'll be there soon."

People had gone to work early or were going to work late. Shops closed for many reasons, such as festivals unrelated to Edmund and his life.

Adjusting the satchel on his shoulder, Edmund wandered, listening for the sounds of anyone coming onto the platform or a train coming towards him, remembering the chores waiting for him at the office. Candice might've finished eating breakfast with her friends, or might still be talking about him. If she would not meet him that evening at Descartes' then he would remain working at his office, trying not to think too much about her. The hands of the platform clock turned with time but nothing else around him moved, until a grey rat scurried along the side of the tracks, hiding from the view of no one there.

Most people were somewhere doing something that sunlit morning, while Edmund walked alone inside an empty station. He again took his telephone, dialled the office number, and heard the recorded message start telling him the office was unattended.

Cautiously, he activated the number of Candice's mobile telephone, programmed among the numbers memorised in his telephone. "Candice Donnelly," spoke her cheerful recorded greeting. "I can't take your call, but please leave me a message and your number."

"Edmund here, checking that I'm seeing you for dinner tonight. I'll try again later." He ended the connection, wondering whether she would telephone him in reply.

He dialled the number of her office, heard her formal recorded voice start telling she wasn't at her desk or was on a telephone call, and ended the connection. He didn't want to seem to be harassing her.

Edmund didn't memorise telephone numbers. The only numbers he could dial were those programmed into his telephone. Some telephones rang, without answer, until he ended the connections. Some diverted his call to other telephones, which rang without reply or which invited him to leave more messages. "Edmund Neale calling," he said, becoming less careful with his words. "It's been much too long since we last spoke, but is something happening today? Please get back to me on this number when you can. Thanks."

He hadn't spoken with most of the people he called friends for many months or years, presuming their friendships endured without it. When they talked, they talked about facets of their work, complaining about the people to whom they each reported.

Edmund again dialled the number of his office, hearing the message telling him that nobody was there; the people working on a public holiday weren't answering the telephone. He again waited for the tone at which he could leave another message. "Hi, June, it's me again, Edmund. Something's wrong with the trains. Can you please give me a call as soon as you get in? Thanks."

He telephoned every person he knew without hearing anyone alive, among the eternity of recorded voices. The display screen on his telephone would've told him if anyone had called him and if any messages were waiting, but still he dialled the number to access the message bank. The computer voice told him he couldn't access it at that time. It suggested he try again later.

Edmund walked around the platform, his satchel hanging from his shoulder. Minutes passed without change, without activity from anyone but him. He was waiting for a train to save him from wondering what to do, but he no longer expected one to come; the monitors above the platform ought to have denoted all the services as being cancelled. The upward escalators started to move as he drifted towards them. They carried him away, but his vantage from the rising stairs over the platforms didn't reveal anything to him.

He ambled back to the barricades, uneasy with the disturbance to the patterns of his life. He could've stepped through the open gate, but instead he stepped towards the turnstiles marked for people leaving the platforms. Waving his travel card by the sensor, his action and the reaction by the turnstile opening before him was a brief semblance of routine in a morning where other routines failed.

The clear sky heralded no evidence of danger. The sun had risen since first Edmund walked outside, shortening the shadows of city buildings. Nothing else had changed. Blinds and curtains across apartment windows might've concealed people, unwilling to stand at the open squares of glass. Some birds made rarefied sounds, beautiful, perhaps, he hadn't heard on other days. The day was weird, surreal, and had come upon him without warning he'd seen or heard; his wisdom could not explain so confounded a morning. A speckle of a doubt appeared in all the things he knew, without facts or reason to excuse it.

Walking back towards his home, his sunglasses back across his eyes, suddenly not knowing what to do, Edmund began to run. He ran as men in suits didn't normally run: his leather-soled shoes almost slipping on the footpath, holding his satchel strap against his shoulder so it wouldn't fall. At the street crossing, he held his right arm out for the traffic lights pole to hold and balance him, looked up and down the empty streets, and resumed running.

3

NEWS

Edmund rushed back up the stairs from the footpath to the building in which he lived, too soon after he'd left it for the day. His key into the lock opened the front door, as it had done every other day. Emptiness in the foyer was commonplace as it wasn't in the streets behind him. The building air was motionless and mild as it was every day, while the front door closed and locked behind him. The lift doors opened immediately when he pressed the button on the wall beside them; he might've been the last person to use them.

He unlocked the door to his apartment and dropped his satchel on the floor inside the door. The numerical electronic display on his telephone answering machine still read "0." The time was slipping after nine o'clock and his crystal carriage clock was softly ticking, when that falsely normal morning might've been its day to stop.

Noise and images of static again filled the screen of his television set and Edmund quickly switched it off. The radio played music from small speakers around the walls: ordinary, soothing, and familiar. The sounds of every morning rested him, while he changed the station to try to find a news report. He pressed the tuning buttons advancing the reception through every frequency and band, but most stations that normally broadcast weren't doing so. He heard more sounds of recorded music and waited impatiently for the song to finish, when somebody alive might talk to him.

The song ended. A recorded advertisement for dishwashing powder played; live human voices would not interrupt advertisements. Another song started.

The first station played a recorded advertisement for soft drink. Another song started. Edmund stopped listening.

The room that could've been a second bedroom was Edmund's private study: his workplace at home, which visitors didn't enter and few girlfriends had seen. Distinguishing his home from the offices in which he worked, the coloured ribbons and minor trophies he received for playing college competition racquetball lay on two high shelves; he'd not played racquetball for years. The room contained no other decorations, no reckless aesthetics.

Edmund's cushioned chair and desk from many years was his only old furniture. Filed in the lowest drawer of his desk were his certificates as old as one for good spelling in kindergarten, rewards that he retained, along with half-yearly reports of his private pension fund. Several textbooks of business and industry, like those in his office, stood tall in a lower set of shelves beside the desk. Books of fact unrelated to his vocation and novels he'd never read stood neatly beside them.

Computers were Edmund's foremost access to the world. The usual programme symbols and responsible icons in their organised array filled the monitor screen before him. No electronic mail had come, although it rarely came to his private home address. Typing his specific password, Edmund accessed mail addressed to him at work. No messages had come to him that morning.

Edmund accessed the international network of computer sites: the Internet. Computers were the world and people with opinions to express, which almost everybody did, with news services in one place much like those in others: the same local news in different circumstances and same world news and current commentary.

Local news services reported the politics, sport, and other

commerce they'd reported yesterday, assuring him the world could not have ended. Each day, Edmund ran his eyes across the headlines and read the opening paragraphs probably important for him to know, until they bored him. The chairman of the Federal Reserve Bank told an audience in Washington that American interest rates weren't high enough to moderate consumer demand. Bandits murdered fourteen German tourists at a resort in South East Asia. A meeting of trade ministers was underway in Melbourne.

Advertisements for commercial product intermittently appeared across the screen, which Edmund closed before their effect was more than just subliminal. He paused briefly at the holiday image of island sands and waters, before closing it.

Expert analyses were those made yesterday, without reason to believe that Tuesday would be anything but normal. The weather would be cool, without rain.

Edmund attempted to access international news services, which might report news about his city so significant as to empty the streets around his home. The screen flickered, producing a standard message: "*The page cannot be found. The page you are looking for might have been removed, had its name changed, or is temporarily unavailable.*"

He couldn't access anything beyond the city in which he lived. The glitch might have been in a single computer hub or server, in which event he'd learn more at his office, or in the communication lines out of the city. He'd mastered technology without knowing much about it.

The news the taxi driver mentioned the previous night might've pertained to the reason Edmund hadn't seen anyone that morning. The driver might've been annoyed that Edmund hadn't let him talk or had challenged him about the route. He might've remained quiet about a warning he'd given other passengers.

Edmund again checked his mobile telephone. Scrolled before him on the small screen were the names of people whose numbers he'd saved there. Among the people he called his friends were those he'd come across by chance and recognised from his student days or past employment. "Edmund?"

"Stephen?"

"What are you doing now?"

"What are you doing now?"

"We must catch up again, soon." They exchanged each other's telephone numbers, carefully writing them on scrap paper or entering them in electronic organisers, and promised to contact each other in quiet moments.

That morning was a quiet moment. The numbers rang but didn't answer before expiring.

Edmund didn't try to contact business acquaintances he knew only through his work. He would not admit to them he didn't know what was happening that day.

The last person he called was his widowed mother, living far away. Like other numbers he'd dialled, the number of her home rang without reply. Edmund wondered whether she'd tried to contact him.

Turning back to his computer on his desk, Edmund typed: "*If you see this message today, please call me.*" His signature appended automatically to his electronic mail included his mobile telephone number and electronic mail address. Appending a request that the computer reading it acknowledge its receipt, Edmund sent his message to every friend whose mail address was programmed in his computer, before his head slumped in his hands.

Hearing the sounds of music playing from the radio, Edmund might've been a fool to think so much about the strangeness that morning. The work his to do was there for any day, among the files and systems of his office; Edmund could work at his office as well as he could sit alone in his apartment. He would see people in the city who could tell him what was happening, and leave the office when Candice telephoned him, if he had reason to go.

Edmund switched off the radio and recovered his satchel from the floor. His sunglasses and mobile telephone in his pockets, he locked the door to his apartment fast. There he hesitated, studying the other apartment doors along the corridor.

Those cream-painted timber doors were almost identical to his, save only for the numbers marking them and the occasional turns of personal taste: a brass knocker, a thimble for fabric flowers. Living in an apartment adjoining his were a married man and woman in suited occupations with their infant baby child. They'd smiled whenever he saw them and wished Edmund a good day or night, but he could not recall their names.

Edmund pressed the button to chime a sound inside their home. He knocked the back of his fingers on the door to supplement it. He watched the blurred light through the peephole in the door for a shadow moving across it and listened for the sound of anybody coming, embarrassed to be doing so. Edmund again pressed the button, before stepping along the corridor to the adjoining like apartment.

Residents might've been sleeping soundlessly in their beds. They might've left their homes before Edmund woke that morning; he could only surmise their reasons for doing so. He knew nothing about them. They knew nothing about him.

Edmund pressed every button and knocked on every door along the corridor, trying to summon anyone. Corporate vice-presidents didn't need to feel embarrassed he thought, before calling out: "Hello, strangers!" If nobody heard him then nobody cared. "Are you there?" Edmund thought of knocking on the doors of other floors in the building, but all the floors of strangers were the same to him. They could've been anywhere doing anything, without interest in him.

The lift was waiting where Edmund left it. He took it to the basement of the building.

A suddenly large space, the car park was empty, but for two left-lonely cars: his dark green sedan parked beside a concrete pillar and a single black car whose owner Edmund didn't know. Touching the ceiling was a blue balloon, its long string handle hanging motionlessly below it. Edmund stared at it, walking slowly towards it. If a child were playing with it then he or she would appear around a pillar. Edmund took the string in his hand, pulling it down like a lever opening a door, but only the balloon came towards him. He examined it, touching its smooth, taut, plastic face. His clean fingers squeaked against the blue, but it was just a balloon. His hand released it, and it rose back to the ceiling.

Cars normally filled the garage overnight, before many of them dissipated through the day and returned throughout the day or evening, but never had Edmund seen a day that everyone drove away. He used public transport to commute to work during the week and only drove his car in evenings or on weekends, sometimes driving to the suburbs or countryside. Edmund hadn't entered the garage since Sunday; he'd not seen other people in the building since the weekend. He couldn't know when the cars and residents had left.

Perhaps the building basement shouldn't have surprised him; people who would otherwise have travelled on a train had used their cars that morning. They might've heard news that Edmund hadn't heard about disruptions to normal train services, and their cars might already be crowded into makeshift parking spaces around offices, shops, and factories.

The lights on his car flickered as Edmund pressed the small button on his key ring to unlock the driver's door from a distance. He hung his jacket neatly from a hook above the rear door behind the driver's seat, placed his telephone in the pocket of the driver's door, and sat in the driver's seat. He might've doubted it would do so on that peculiar morning, but the engine to his car started when he turned the key in the ignition switch. The car radio played music from the same two stations that played it from his apartment radios, while the buttons set to other stations produced only static when he pressed them. Pressing the button on a small remote control device clicked the locks and cogs of the garage doors, hauling them open. The settling light of day rose before him.

Sensing his breath escaping from the building, Edmund placed his sunglasses over his eyes. Only habit warranted him pausing before he drove across the footpath to the roadway, looking for pedestrians not on the pavement and moving cars not on the street. The basement doors closed automatically behind him, sealing the building from thieves and vandals.

Edmund drove cautiously towards the city centre, pausing at red traffic lights to look around and not see anything worthwhile. Corners opened up long cross roads and short side streets, as empty as was every other street he'd seen that day.

That working or not-working day, the few cars parked at kerbside parking places were reasons to believe he might find the people who'd driven them or been passengers in them. Edmund stopped his car beside some and saw only daylight through the windows; people rarely sat in cars in sunshine.

Other people might be driving too far ahead for him to see them or on other roads, thinking the same thoughts that he was thinking, searching for him. His eyes glanced at the rear-vision mirror but he couldn't see them in reflection. From the radio came a recorded advertisement for yoga and other relaxation therapies, before the music resumed.

Every block of buildings past which he drove was one more likely to herald moving cars, people, or open shopfront doors, but the streets and footpaths remained destitute. The stores, bars, and restaurants were closed. Not even the beggars were there, sitting on their wooden crates or cardboard mats and accepting bags of food from people who hadn't eaten all their meals.

People often congregated in the shopping mall or mulled near cinemas and theatres, but they too were deserted. Only birds meandered on the sun-blessed parks of trees and lawns; nobody jogged along the paths or played soccer on the grass, or reclined on wooden benches eating sandwiches. Edmund didn't understand the significance of anything he saw or the people he didn't see. Suddenly an alien in a strange place he'd always known, he didn't know far more than he knew.

Driving too easily, without traffic or pedestrians obstructing him, his solitude in places he'd only seen with crowds became beguiling. The traffic lights shone red at some intersections, where Edmund stopped and waited for no cars to pass and for the lights to change; the first car he saw that day shouldn't be one crashing into him, the first person shouldn't be a police officer deducting demerit points from his driver licence and fining him. Cameras at several intersections photographed the registration plates of cars travelling past red lights, and only his deference to scrutiny he couldn't see constrained Edmund as he drove. The mesmerising mystery of the day became more profound with the growing emptiness.

The roads and footpaths crowded yesterday were desolate. The stalls along the footpaths and shops at the feet of many buildings were closed behind their doors and shutters. Security locks sealed most city buildings, but the glass doors and building fronts could've revealed a cleaner, security guard, or other person working. No remnant of a human life was there, in the place where people could only be. That hub of their activities was bereft of everything but Edmund in his slowly moving car.

He veered his car towards the kerb and parked outside the building in which he worked, glad to park so easily without recourse to a commercial parking station. (For almost two years, he'd waited for the next available corporate parking space.) Edmund stopped the engine, while keeping the radio alive just loud enough for him to hear an interrupting voice. A recorded advertisement promoted financial services, before the recorded music resumed.

Buildings of office windows looked down upon him, without anyone that he could see among them. Fluorescent lights shone from the ceilings of intermittent floors, although they might've been the lights that shone last night, when other floors were dark. People at their desks would be invisible below the windows. Edmund blasted his car horn summoning them to the street. No one appeared. Edmund could not be certain that anyone was there.

Edmund sat alone, his car obvious and oblivious among the barren streets and buildings. He removed his sunglasses from his eyes to see nothing there more clearly. Soon after Sunday dawn, the city might be so empty, but not half an hour past nine o'clock on another Tuesday morning. He wondered whether to worry, without knowing about what.

He dialled the number of his apartment, ready to enter the code to access messages left for him, but no messages were there. The telephone directory information service didn't answer.

Edmund was reticent to dial the emergency number without needing the police, ambulance, or fire brigade, but the number rang without reply for more than a minute before he ended the connection. The circumstances in which the emergency services didn't answer were difficult to imagine, unless all the operators were engaged on other calls from people who'd woken into the empty city or a computer malfunction affected them.

If sirens wailing through the streets had ordered people to evacuate the city then they would've disturbed his office concentration Monday evening or woken him through the night, no matter how deeply he slept. He would've seen someone running through the streets or driving fast away.

If everyone but he had fled for the suburbs or the country then perhaps he too should flee, but they'd gone so many hours earlier. People might've fled before a virus or bacteria killed them in their beds, but it hadn't killed Edmund asleep in his or left corpses in the streets. Sick people might be crowded into hospitals, but Edmund hadn't fallen sick. He felt well, without anybody near him.

The owners of cars parked at the kerbs might've been the only people to remain, although they might've been passengers in cars their friends and relatives drove or been passengers on trains or buses. People in their homes might be transfixed by emptiness or too frightened to leave, huddled where Edmund hadn't seen them. Edmund might be the only person left vulnerable, sitting alone in his small car.

What sudden news might he alone have missed? The news might've been good or bad, enticing everyone to witness something or forcing everyone to flee: an industrial accident at a nuclear reactor or chemical plant, a pending earthquake or other environmental danger, poison in the water.

His car windows were closed; clouds of radiation might be transparent. Edmund studied the outside air for patterns, shades, or colours not normally there, without knowing the anomalies for which to look or the features he might find. He tried to taste an odour in the air inside his car, ready to cover his nose and mouth if he smelt pollutant. He tried to feel disturbance in his skin, but couldn't sense anything.

A grey pigeon rested on a street light, uninterested in him. The bird might've arrived since a disaster or already been in the city, but its survival was also his. Edmund softly pressed the button in his car door armrest, narrowly opening the window beside him. The cool outside air didn't seem to harm him; it felt safe enough to breathe. He couldn't discern any aroma, but didn't know if aroma was normally there. Never before had he thought to taste the air.

If terrorists threatening to eradicate the city had taken control of all but two radio stations then those two stations would've broadcast warnings to the populace, instead of music and advertisements for things he didn't want. Edmund's only images of their carnage were from news and documentary: the falling towers of the World Trade Centre against blue skies in New York. His knowledge of grand events and cruel disasters in other times and places was too scant for him to know what he would see if a new war threatened. Wars were the reports of foreign correspondents for which people fretted but never feared; people who'd not stood among the ruins of a war zone or seen a body dead had stopped contemplating wars in their safe bits of earth. If a war were coming then the army would defend him, but no helicopters flew above or trucks drove along the streets.

Nothing came from anywhere. Edmund couldn't see or hear a risk of death.

The city of his home was silent, with old and new buildings intact. Electricity flowed, the radio played. Water had come through his apartment taps that morning.

Film-makers conceived aliens landing somewhere on the earth, without convincing Edmund that they would. Solar flares might distort radio and television signals, but not kill anyone. Too much carbon or too little ozone would harm birds and lesser animals before people, in centuries to come.

The threats he'd postulated were incredulous, but so too was that morning. Something beyond extraordinary had led everyone away. His imagination was his ignorance: too much the product of horror and adventure movies. He leant forward and looked up through the car windscreen between the building tops towards the sky, where the trail of a high-flying aeroplane disappeared from view. Edmund turned his mind back to reality around him.

Nothing around him explained his solitude. In spite of everything that morning, he could not imagine disaster looming to ward everyone away. He didn't believe that terrorists would do to him what they'd done to the people of New York the day the towers fell.

Edmund switched off the radio and listened to the streets. Perhaps he should've heard birds singing or dogs barking, but he'd never before listened for them. Any other day, he wouldn't have noticed the pigeon resting on the light. He didn't know what he should hear, or see, in the city without people. The pigeon flew away.

4

MISSING PEOPLE

The time was after ten o'clock. The radio was reason to believe the day was an ordinary day, in its important respects.

Edmund might've been a fool for noticing he'd not seen anyone. The chance that everyone was elsewhere might just have been another possibility along a distribution curve of possibilities, one more permutation to occur; statistics were tiny summaries of everything that had transpired. Other people could've been living that day as he lived it: sitting in their cars not having heard the news, looking out from windows he couldn't see. The city was a metropolis and he, by an extraordinary coincidence of the choices that other people made, hadn't come across them. People might've left the city without universal reason before he woke that morning. Remnants of the populace roaming the city might've wandered along footpaths he wasn't passing when they did. He would draw no inferences, reach no conclusions, but live as he always lived until he knew otherwise. Aloneness in a place for crowds needed merely to intrigue him.

He would see people soon enough. Sometime somebody would hear or read a message he'd left and contact him. Taking comfort from that reason for Candice not responding, he would call her again later, when she would tell him she would meet him at the restaurant or say something less to mean that she would not.

Only his chores remained; those always there. Work didn't cease to be important because people weren't there; the tasks waiting for him at his office would again be paramount when everyone returned. Edmund could work while other people didn't and fare better for having done so, attracting Hugh Garrett's attention and respect; ambitious aspirants sought new tasks to undertake. Later, while others struggled, it would afford him time with Candice.

Edmund placed his sunglasses back over his eyes and raised the car door window beside him. Removing his keys from the ignition lock, he stepped outside, taking his jacket, mobile telephone, and satchel with him. He pressed the button on his key ring and heard the locks of the car doors click down; the headlights and taillights flickered. Without parking police prepared to fine him patrolling the street, he left alone the machine at which people paid to park along the kerb.

The thick-glass double doors at the building entrance opened automatically when anyone approached them during normal working hours on normal working days, after somebody had set them. They remained closed as Edmund strode towards them that Tuesday morning. On the wall beside the doors was a groove along which he slid his work security card. The doors opened, and closed again after he entered the building.

Edmund's security card activated the sensor in the lift into which he stepped, before he pressed the third-floor button; Edmund's card didn't give him access to other floors. Standing alone in a rising lift, without stopping at other floors for other people, was normal on public holidays. "Level three," said the electronic female voice from the speakers in the lift, a rare voice addressing him that day.

The lift doors opened. Edmund stepped into the silent floor. Ceiling lights around the lifts shone down and the green exit signs to the fire stairs were bright, but the company offices beyond the closed door and a glass wall were dark, as they'd been when Edmund left them Monday night. No morning newspapers or magazines lay on the floor outside office doors, waiting for secretaries to carry them into offices. The lift doors closed behind him; the building lifts were programmed to return to the ground floor.

Edmund's keys unlocked the door to the company reception area, with its black leather waiting chairs, shining plants, and coffee table offering industry magazines. The bank of black plastic switches on one wall clicked alive the long fluorescent lights in the ceiling above him, around the reception desk, and throughout the offices. His security card admitted him through another door before the door sprang closed behind him.

Hugh Garrett wasn't in his office. Edmund walked along each corridor, peering through each glass wall and open doorway, onto empty desks behind low partitions, looking for anyone at work. The kitchen and stationery room were as empty of people as was every other corner of the offices.

Edmund's diary didn't identify any public holiday or commemoration that day or any appointments by which he could quiz the people he'd agreed to see, save one. "*7 pm. Candice, Descartes'. Be there!!*"

Activating his computer, the usual symbols and corporate motifs filled the screen. Edmund typed his name and password on the keyboard, allowing him access to the network server. No new electronic messages had come. The local news services, everything ordinary, remained unchanged since last he looked at them, without any breaking stories. Nobody had anything to say, nothing new to be the news, as nobody might on the most pervasive of public holidays. Technical problems or industrial disputes might've caused the lack of journalistic work that day, as they might have disrupted other commerce. News services from beyond the city in which he lived remained inaccessible to him.

Affixed to a corkboard on the wall was a list of telephone numbers for company employees. Edmund started to dial Hugh Garrett's mobile telephone number, before realising he would appear foolish for contacting him without good cause. He pressed his finger on the button pre-emptively ending the connection, and dialled the number of a colleague with whom he could speak more freely. The telephone rang for a long time, before the answering machine began playing the outgoing recorded message; people leaving their homes normally activated their answering machines to play after only a few rings. "Hello Paul, Edmund Neale. I'm at the office. Please call me when you can. Thanks."

A button on his telephone base-set activated a radio, and Edmund heard the recurring recorded music and an advertisement assuring him he had no cause to fear. Referring to the computer telephone directory, he dialled the number of the radio station. "This office is currently unattended," answered another recorded voice. "Please call us again during normal business hours when someone would be pleased to speak with you. Thank you." The number had been to an unoccupied administrative section, much like the offices in which he sat.

Edmund left messages for several of his colleagues, some of whom might be working in their homes, before becoming weary of the exercise. Not wanting too many people responding, he ended the connections without reciting messages. He turned again to the chairman's telephone number, collecting his breath and rehearsing his words. "You have called Hugh Garrett," replied the answering service. "You may leave a message after the tone."

"Good morning, Mister Garrett. Edmund Neale here, at the office, checking you received the submission I sent you last night. That was all. Thank you."

The spring water cooler in the kitchen was half full. The percolator on the bench contained the last cold coffee that Edmund had not consumed when it was warm, late Monday night. Hugh Garrett's personal assistant had affixed a small sewn image of a bear to the noticeboard, asking: "*Is there life before coffee?*" She could've asked the same question of tea, when good coffee was unavailable.

Edmund took a mug from the high cupboard, dropped into it a teabag, and held it under the dispenser heating water from the taps. From an airtight plastic Tupperware container, he took two chocolate chip biscuits, leaving other varieties behind. Giving the tea time to brew, Edmund read the colourful postcards some secretaries sent the office from their holidays. Relaxed at work as he only could alone, he dropped the teabag in the rubbish bin.

Weekends and public holidays were times to work comfortably and expeditiously, without people at his door, telephones ringing, or so much electronic mail; Hugh Garrett expected him to work at least some public holidays. Nobody would interrupt him, until the people came to work. The curious non-events that morning would not distract him.

Edmund perused the papers on his desk and correspondence in his computer, occasionally responding, sometimes sipping tea and nibbling another corner of a slowly shrinking biscuit. He read photocopied circulars at which he'd previously glanced just long enough to know he need not consider them immediately and approved payment of invoices. At the corner of his desk closest to the door was a short stack of black plastic trays, from the middle of which he took incoming papers and into the uppermost of which he placed the work his secretary would quietly collect. He dictated correspondence into his hand-held recording machine and left the cassette tapes for her to play later at her desk, sometimes misunderstanding the words he meant to say. He composed the terms for a joint venture with another company, when writing words on paper was easier than trying to recite them from his head. He deliberated upon his reasoning and research, until satisfied with what he had accomplished.

The longer tasks Edmund noted in his time sheets that most employees completed, allocating costs and revenue. His work accorded him mental occupation and he chided himself before losing time to concentration, but the city emptiness increasingly distracted him. The chair in which he sat was on small canister wheels. He pulled it the short way along the carpet until his face was near the window. The trees along the footpaths stood like sentinels beside the empty street, save only for his car parked alone against the kerb. A few more leaves might've fallen and settled on the ground, but nothing material had changed since he arrived. No parking policeman had left a ticket under a windscreen wiper of his car.

He had no reason to sit and wonder from silent office

windows. Edmund broke between chores concocted on his desk to stretch his back and legs, prepare fresh mugs of tea, and drop the plastic wrapper from a fresh packet of biscuits in the kitchen garbage bin. He left notes of tasks for clerks on their sedentary workstations and took sweets for everyone's consumption from June's glass jar on her desk. Without conversations to perform, he paused at the open door to Mister Garrett's office. Memories of people could be vivid without them present to confuse him.

Edmund's promotion to a vice presidency two years earlier had been the most exciting moment of his life, when the chairman brought him into his office and warmly shook his hands. "People who called you 'Edmund' yesterday will call you 'Mister Neale' today," Hugh Garrett smiled. "Some who called you 'Mister Neale' will now want to call you 'Edmund'."

Edmund nodded, being led through his induction.

"But you will continue to call me Mister Garrett, and I will continue to call you whatever I feel like calling you."

Uncertain whether to smile, Edmund nodded earnestly.

"Most importantly, Edmund, you must never become complacent. Poverty is ugly, and relative poverty is relatively ugly."

Edmund was still enjoying his new title on his thirty-second birthday, when the chairman summoned him to his office. Reading a document Edmund had drafted, Garrett shook his head. Look, Neale," he said, "I want this paper to include reference to automation. Working without people; that's the future." Garrett clenched his fist and held it above his desk. "I'm not sure you're the right person for this." Garrett dropped Edmund's work in the bin beneath his desk.

"I'll rectify it, Mister Garrett," said Edmund. "If you can wait until nine o'clock tomorrow morning, I'll give you what you want."

The chairman studied him, before nodding. He clicked his fingers twice in quick succession, ushering Edmund to his task.

Edmund cancelled his dinner engagement and remained late at his desk. He returned there early in the morning, resumed redrafting, and resubmitted his paper to the chairman as their office clocks touched nine o'clock. Edmund again sat facing him, reading Edmund's work. "I was wrong, Edmund," smiled Garrett, finishing the last paragraph, laying the paper gently on his desk, and looking across at Edmund. "You might be the right person, after all." Edmund restrained himself from smiling in his presence.

Returning from his musings to the present, that stillborn Tuesday morning, Edmund sat at Garrett's desk. His ears pricked high for the sound of someone entering the offices, Edmund pressed a keyboard button. Appearing on the screen was a security window wanting him to type a name and password. In the same format as his login name, he typed "*hgarrett*". Guessing the chairman's password, he typed the name of Garrett's wife: "*Delores*".

The computer asked him to check the spelling. His guess was incorrect.

Edmund dared not guess again, for fear another error froze the computer. He switched it off, leaving no evidence he'd been there.

Shortly before one o'clock, when most employees were normally preparing for lunch, Edmund stacked his mug in the kitchen dishwasher and took a final biscuit to chew. Dressed back into his jacket, carrying his satchel, and donning his sunglasses, he switched off the office lights and locked the office door behind him, as if the day were any other in which he was the last to leave.

"Ground floor," the electronic lady of the lift bid him well. A button opened the glass doors, releasing him from the building. Edmund's car radio played an advertisement for holidays to escape from hectic crowds.

The offices in which Candice worked were much like those where Edmund worked, in a building several blocks away that could've been the same. From his car, Edmund imagined waving at her just as she'd threatened to wave at him in his office that evening. Taking his telephone in his hand, Edmund again dialled the number of Candice's mobile telephone.

"Candice Donnelly," her cheerful recorded greeting repeated. "I can't take your call, but please leave me a message and your number."

"Candice, Edmund here. Something strange has happened. Nobody seems to be anywhere. Please call me when you get this message. Thanks."

The premises most likely to be open in spite of an emergency were the central city police station. Edmund preferred to go and find it closed than to wonder if it was.

Outside was a police car, beside which Edmund parked. Electric lights shone throughout the building and the entrance doors opened when he pushed them; a police station into which anyone could walk would not be empty. Spring mechanisms drew the doors closed behind him, restoring the silence in the station.

A long, low wooden counter separated the public area from the desks at which police officers normally sat, with their computer screens turned away from public gaze. A closed wooden gate through the counter admitted people and permitted them to leave the private space beyond it, at the invitation and discretion of police.

"Hello," Edmund called to anybody there. His fingers tapped on the counter while he looked around the doors through which somebody could come. Near him were racks of brochures advising people about driving under the influence of drugs and alcohol and about reporting crime and traffic accidents to police. The brochures portrayed smiling police officers in shining uniforms, but those officers weren't tending to him. "Is anyone there?"

An open station without police was incongruous. So was everything else that day.

"Hello," Edmund called again. "Hello." He walked along the counter front to the wooden gate. "Can I come in?" Edmund's hand pushed the gate, but couldn't move it. He leaned over the gate, saw the bolt sealing it shut, and pulled the bolt through its latch. "Hello?" Tentatively, he pushed open the gate, leaving the sanctuary of a place that he could lawfully be. "Hello?"

Fearing someone misconstruing his actions, Edmund prepared his excuse. "I called out," he said, "but nobody was here."

Most computer screens were dark, but the police department

forceful logo shone from two of them. If their last users had left their desks without deactivating them, the computers had switched automatically into power-saving modes.

A mug of white coffee and a Bible lay on a desk by one computer. The mug was cold.

Edmund slowly pushed open a door and entered a corridor. "Hello," he called out. More doors opened when he turned the handles, revealing offices with desks and empty chairs. If not a human being, then he hoped to find a cup of still warm coffee, an active computer terminal, or a pen on paper in the midst of composition.

Gently tapping his knuckles so not to seem demanding, Edmund knocked on the closed door of the men's washroom. "Excuse me, please," he said, loudly enough for his voice to transcend however many doors separated him from a cubicle. "Is anyone there?"

No sounds reached back to him. A stranger had more reason to enter a washroom than to enter offices, but hesitantly Edmund pushed open the door. Nobody stood at the white porcelain urinal. The grey door to the only cubicle was open. Nobody was there. Edmund ran the tip of his index finger around the washbasin drainage hole and it was dry.

His knuckles knocked more loudly on the door of the adjoining women's washroom and then knocked on it again. "Excuse me, please," he called out. He waited for a response much longer than he'd waited at the door of the men's washroom. "Is anyone in there?" He left the door alone.

Holding cells were for people arrested on minor charges held no longer than overnight. Inside the room with iron bars across the windows, both cells were empty. Anyone alive or dying on the floor and Edmund could've saved each other, but Edmund was the only prisoner in custody.

The kitchen and recreation area contained an old television set, which Edmund activated. Static filled the screen and noise scratched from the speakers without varying between channels, confirming what he'd already known. Resting on a table was a radio he switched on, and heard a recorded advertisement for hypnotherapy.

A board of notices didn't include any press release or explanation of where everyone had gone. Covering most of the board were photographs of missing people, criminals, and suspected criminals, at which Edmund's eyes stared and whose eyes stared back at him, while a song of unrequited love began behind him. Young, middle-aged, and elderly, they were the first new faces he'd seen that day, with names and other particulars he didn't need to know. They were tall, of average height, and short, with eyes and hair of different shades and colour: a microcosm of the city yesterday.

The captions for missing people included the date, place, and brief circumstances of their disappearance, many weeks, months, and years earlier. The police held grave fears for their safety. Some had histories of mental illness. Perhaps Edmund was accumulating such a history for himself.

A photograph of Candice should've been among the faces on the board, the first and most beautiful displayed, as should've photographs of his near and far acquaintances and every other city resident. Edmund alone remained to report them missing, wherever they had gone. He had too little to report, except their disappearance had happened overnight.

The legacies of human lives around him made Edmund try to conceive a catastrophe obliterating people in the middle of their moments without damaging their cars and buildings, but he couldn't comprehend such a calamity. He didn't think it possible. If people vanished in a whiff of science fiction fantasy, then dead man's handles would stop moving trains and automatic pilots would land flying aircraft, but the cars that people drove would crash across the roads. There were always people in their cars, even in the earliest moments of the quietest dark mornings. Remembering each crazy thought just made it desperate in his brain, but reason hadn't taught him anything that day. His imaginings were foolish and fanciful: his mind meandering without another place to go.

Leaning back against the wall, he faced where he shouldn't have been: a private police area in the largest station in the city. A burly police officer hearing the radio might come through a door and brusquely ask the brazen stranger, "What are you doing here?"

Edmund's business shirt and tie would assure the officer he wasn't dangerous, but Edmund turned his hands from his side so the officer would not draw his gun in self-defence. "The station was open," Edmund would respond. "I was concerned."

He couldn't imagine any more words of conversation between them. The officer might warn him to leave the city, or might escort him to the streets where the strangers soon would be. The song finished playing from the radio.

Closed doors didn't open. Shadows through open doorways didn't move. The station remained silent, the only voices those trapped in Edmund's reckless imagination.

The silence continued: silence, where there ought to have been music or advertisements. Edmund turned to the radio set, stepped towards it, and reached it as the silence became static. Pressing the button to change the reception frequency, the light and electronic display raced through numbers of frequencies searching for a signal. The number stopped where an advertisement for relationship counselling came from the radio. Edmund again pressed the tuning button and the light and electronic display raced upward until it reached the high end of its range and started again at the low end, before the advertisement resumed. Only one station still broadcast.

5

THE RADIO STATION

Not wanting to be a lost victim of a disaster he'd never noticed, Edmund ran back along the corridors of the police station to the open area of desks and through the counter wooden gate. Soldiers would've responded to any threat for which police were inadequately equipped, but might've not arrived because the danger wasn't over.

Edmund started the engine of his car. The radio played a recorded advertisement for hair gel.

The radio station still broadcasting occupied a three-storey building, from which the station logo shone in sunlight. A car stood in a space marked for employees, beside which Edmund parked. He pushed open the door.

Dominating the lobby was a high desk at which Edmund imagined a security guard or receptionist normally sitting. Behind the desk was a television monitor with images of empty corridors. Edmund proceeded to the lift, pressed the button to take him upwards, and waited. The lift doors opened and he stepped inside, without knowing where he'd find the origin of the broadcast. The first floor was any place to start.

Edmund stepped from the lift into a silent corridor. Several doors were closed, but he walked to the door nearest him, turned the handle, and opened it. The lightly furnished office was unoccupied.

Leaving that door open so he could hear sounds emanating from anywhere beyond it and so he wouldn't open that door again, he opened the next door along the corridor. The room with several empty chairs pushed into an empty wooden table had been one for meetings. The next door opened to another lightly furnished office, from which one door opened to a cupboard and another to another empty office. Every door stood wide open when Edmund finished exploring the floor of empty rooms.

The lift at the second floor opened to another silent corridor, but with a large multiple-glazed soundproof window in the wall sealing a closed room. Edmund rushed up to the sound-suppressing window, but saw only an empty chair close to a single table. Lying on the table was a microphone and pair of headphones, before a panel of dials, switches, and buttons for use by somebody not there. Among the screens of words and numbers, waves on a monitor moved in unison with waves of little lights: the rising and falling volumes Edmund heard in his car but couldn't hear in the silence of the corridor, staring through the sheets of glass.

Programmers had set the computer to play recorded music and advertisements without relief; years might've passed since the station dispensed with human broadcasters. Programmers, people selling advertising time, and managers didn't need to be there. The sounds of radio implied nothing.

Perhaps, just perhaps, somebody had spoken into the microphone through Monday evening, while Edmund was at work. The radio was the loudest voice still speaking.

Two doors led from the enclosed room, but not into the corridor. Edmund opened the corridor door closest to him and entered another room, from which a door admitted him into the silent broadcast room. He sat in the only chair at the solitary table, before the dials, switches, and buttons. He clasped the headphones to his head, adjusting the silent, cushioned speakers to his ears. The coiled black cord from the headphones entered the panel close to a switch he flicked, jarring him with the sounds of women singing. The volume of their voices accompanied the lights in rising waves.

Edmund couldn't find a button on the microphone, from which another cord led into the panel beside a switch and light marked with an unfamiliar symbol. His fingers were poised to flick that switch, waiting for his mind to determine what to say. Ignorance was a fault and he didn't want to seem concerned or panicked. Too few people would interrupt their time to help him, and he needed to give them reason to find him; his salvation had to be the best interests of the saviours and the saved. He wanted to find people without them knowing he was doing so.

He flicked the switch. Nothing obvious occurred. He flicked another, without response that he detected. Shining lights faded and other lights shone. Nothing else changed. He flicked each switch on the panel, guessing what to do and awaiting any consequence, until the women ceased singing through his ears.

Edmund stopped. "Good afternoon," he spoke into the microphone, his voice in stereo coming through the headphones taking him aback. They let him hear his voice without it resonating through the broadcast. "On this very quiet day, everyone who gathers in the city mall at four o'clock will hear a free concert." The time on the wall clock was almost three. "That's right: a free concert." Even with every other venue closed, music alone mightn't entice them. "Everyone coming to the concert has a chance to win a beautiful Genevan gold watch," Edmund told his virtual audience he hoped was real, becoming reckless in his anonymity. "Everyone will get money. That's right: everyone."

Nobody appeared at the window, protesting what he'd said. He should leave before anybody did.

"We also have a special competition in which a lucky woman can win dinner for two at Descartes' restaurant," Edmund resumed, "but it's only open to women named Candice, forgiving women. I'll play some music by Bach later today, Candice, just for you. So we'll see you all, especially you Candice, four o'clock today, for a free concert, prizes, and money at the mall. Today only; be quick."

Edmund flicked back that final switch. Music again played to his ears from the speakers, he then deactivated. Removing the headphones from his head, he rested them where he'd found them. Resting back in the chair, he wondered whether the station broadcast far enough for her to hear him.

If someone burst through a door, then he would explain his words were just a joke promoting his favourite radio station. In mitigation and excuse, he would tell the police he'd tried to save the people left behind. He wasn't certain which story to tell journalists, who might make him a celebrity for committing deeds for which police would prosecute him.

The room remained silent, until Edmund stood up from the chair. He closed the doors behind him as he left.

The radio was playing music when he again started the engine of his car, without any voice interrupting the usual broadcast to say there was no concert or contest. A recorded voice advertised hair dyes, before another song began to play. The music and advertisements continued.

Thousands of screaming people might shortly gather in the mall, expecting to get money and hear a concert and hoping to win a watch. One or more of them might be hoping to win dinner at Descartes' restaurant, which might appreciate the publicity. Edmund started to smile, imagining the police tending to the mob and radio station apologising for the error it hadn't made, while Edmund finding Candice in the crowd led her away. The story of the broadcast and crowds responding to it would be news in coming days: more soon-forgotten conversations. To Candice he might admit and maybe boast he was the mystery man behind the hoax.

The streets around the mall were like all other streets, with some parked cars but more pigeons dithering about dried leaves and trunks of trees seeking scraps of food, accustomed quickly to people having gone. Without other motions in the mall, a fountain plying water over falls into a pond was a solitary recurrence. In the stores was merchandise he'd worked hard to acquire, but had no time or wealth to buy.

That day for easy parking, Edmund parked his car beside the kerb and sat where he observed the mall. The volume of the sound playing from his radio was low and the window beside him open for him to hear anybody coming, but the gently splashing fountain was the only noise outside.

Edmund adjusted himself, trying to be comfortable. The tips of his fingers tapped each other.

Thirty minutes would elapse before the concert was scheduled not to start. Edmund studied the streets, searching for what he hadn't seen that day: a car moving from a kerb, a bicycle coming around a corner. He studied the scene as if something might change because he did: a door opening, movement at a window. Building windows didn't reveal a person watching him, although the sun and sky reflected from the highest glass obscured his vision of the space beyond them. The city didn't change for him thinking so much about it.

The streets were peaceful without people, without pedestrians hurrying between queues, their origins and destinations all alike, and the clutter of loud cars moving too slowly for impatient people trapped inside them, jostling with each other for places left to park. They reflected something unerringly elegant, as the architects and town planners once wanted cities to be: art forms he'd never paused to realise. Edmund did not disturb the silence and serenity.

The dinner engagement he cancelled the night he saved his job, his thirty-second birthday, had been with Geomie, his fiancée, whose words and his replies might sound again when next he spoke with Candice. Geomie was asleep when Edmund returned to their apartment and remained asleep while he continued working at his computer. He returned to their apartment the next evening with his job intact, but Geomie gone, as had her clothes and everything else she'd brought there. Only her engagement ring remained, sitting on the glass of a grey table.

Edmund dialled her mobile telephone, but it didn't respond. He would've dialled the numbers of her friends' homes, but he didn't know them. In the morning, he dialled the number of her work, but spoke only to a recording machine. "What's going on, Geomie?" he asked. "If you're there, please pick up the telephone. I'll be at the office all day and at home this evening."

Geomie telephoned him at his apartment that evening. "I haven't been happy for a long time," she explained. "We shared a home to spend more time together, but you never noticed that we didn't. Everywhere I walked I was content, until I returned to our apartment where I was lonely."

"You should've told me."

"I did tell you, but you were thinking about something else. We weren't a couple. We were a convenience, whenever you could fit us in between appointments."

"My life is more complicated than you realise," said Edmund. "I can't allow relationships to affect my work."

"I don't allow work to affect my relationships, not my important ones. Work ought to be a place to produce to make somebody happy. For you, it's somewhere to belong."

"I can't afford to lose my job," he explained. "Poverty is ugly, and relative poverty is relatively ugly."

"Who do you know is poor?" Geomie rebutted him. "Who with a home in which to live, food to eat, clothes to wear, is poor?"

"I want more than that."

"So do I," she said, their parting conversation concluded.

During a Sunday afternoon he would've shared with her, Edmund, one among the many, wandered about the stores; his was a material world. Happy people didn't notice him, just another person spending money, but he noticed all of them, until the shop display windows exhibiting merchandise curiously consoled him. Reflected in the shining red and glass of a small model Porsche sports car, when he held his head at the right angle, he could almost see his face. Something worthwhile was intrinsic in the work he did whether or not Geomie understood it, and whether or not he always understood it. Meeting women except in transit was difficult, becoming involved with those with whom he worked too great a complication when the relationship expired. Fearing he might never fare better than he'd already fared, never feel again what he'd felt, he sold the engagement ring back to the shop from which he bought it.

Two years later, the model car lay on a shelf in Edmund's office, among the textbooks, journals, and seminar papers to which he occasionally referred. The glass and metalwork had dulled; office cleaners wiping dust from shelves didn't clean personal items. The peripheries of his lifestyle had been his distraction from work and his rationale for doing so, but the baits that once enticed him from the edges of his career served only to tease him; they were too far away for him to touch. Among a constancy of constants, the only variations to a theme were in the women whom he knew and almost knew, passing through his lesser hours of life.

Edmund turned the key out of the ignition switch, stopping the radio. He opened the door beside him and stepped outside, where the air was cooler than it had been inside his car. The only sounds reaching his ears remained the fountain water.

Walking around the mall, pigeons skipped away from him, opening the ground around him in a wake from grey and white. Without the chaos of congestion, he'd become conspicuous. The emptiness that accentuated the city art and scenery also accentuated Edmund, without anyone but God and him to see his accentuated self. He was the focal dot along the streets of shades of grey mapped out around him.

Strangers in the city didn't speak, but Edmund would approach anyone he saw and make unthreatening conversation. "Not many people in the city today," he would casually observe, hoping the stranger would tell him the reason instead of simply being uneasy that Edmund had said anything. "Do you know where everyone is?" He wanted to know the truth without embarrassing himself by asking.

The stranger might mutter something. He might not know the answer, or not express the answer to him.

Any exchange would be easier if the stranger first asked Edmund why he'd remained. He or she might be a police officer, warning him to leave.

The time was almost four. Edmund again sat in his car, while the radio whispered recorded music and advertisements to which he wasn't listening.

He might've been asleep, dreaming memories of a day that never was. He concentrated his eyes and mind through the windscreen to patterns in the light, trying to force changes in what he saw as he only could in dreams. They didn't change. The streets had detail that dreams did not provide: lines of buildings, doors, and windows; etches in the poles and footpaths. The city was quieter than simply dreaming could've made it.

Edmund reached out his hand until his outstretched fingers touched the windscreen. The glass was cold and smooth, senses to his skin. He placed his hand on his chest to feel each of them against the other. He touched his cheeks and pinched his skin in the adage that would've woken him if he felt pain. His brain was feeling, thinking. His thoughts turned upon themselves, convincing Edmund he was awake.

He might have been insane, but didn't know how to determine if he was. The images he saw and had seen that day were real, to him.

Lights shone in some shops and offices but most were dark, shadowed from the sun without lights of their own. The time drifted past four.

Most people didn't listen to the radio. People who did listen to it mightn't have listened to that station, even when it was the only station broadcasting. People listening to his broadcast wouldn't enter every contest or attend every complimentary concert. People coming from the suburbs mightn't have had the time to reach the mall, although they could arrive at any time to an open-air event. The radio began playing another song.

People might've entered the mall without Edmund seeing them from his car, and he again opened the door beside him. The air was colder every time he stepped outside and he held his arms close to his chest. The paths and passageways from the mall stretched away from him, but the only motions were the pigeons pecking at the ground and the splashing water in the small falls of the fountain. The concert he'd not convened was for an audience not there.

No helicopters hovered overhead, warding him away. Edmund closed and locked his car door behind him.

The bubbling fountain, that beacon of lost normalcy, drew him towards it. If Edmund wanted a reason for doing so, then he was searching for people in the shops. His pace quickening, the pigeons scarpering, his shoes soon pounded on the ground. He reached the fountain, stopped, and spun around in empty space: a whirlwind in still air. "Is anybody there?" he screamed, startling more pigeons. In a sudden single flock, they flew into the air.

His words echoed between the shopfronts as they bounced around the mall. "Hello," he screamed, at the people hiding behind doors and windows. "Hello. Hello."

The lives around and not around him flowed inside his brain. Wherever people had all gone, they'd not returned to him.

In the middle of the mall, Edmund pressed his face against a florist's window, held his hands to shield the reflections of the city, and peered through the glass. Flowers picked in bloom ready to be sold that morning had begun to wither; the water in the troughs and buckets not enough to keep them fresh. If anyone cowered on the floor then he or she had hidden well. Edmund pulled his face and hands from the window and turned around. "Come on!" he screamed again, moving along the mall. "Is anybody there?"

Only the water answered. Edmund stood alone in a hollow among hollows. Nobody was coming to rescue him. Perhaps the affliction across that muted space threatened to afflict anyone who came. Too many cities might've been suffering and his city was somewhere late in turn. Perhaps the people in other places didn't know what was happening to his home. Perhaps they didn't care.

Edmund wandered lost and listless about the mall, vulnerable to something he didn't recognise. He longed to comprehend his loss, but knew most of the same nothing he hadn't known that morning. The people might've gone to a better place than that in which he persevered. Far from being the sole survivor, he might've been the only person perishing. Only the birds and maybe he remained.

Of all the people who hadn't come, one mattered most. Edmund drove quickly to the building in which Candice lived, in an apartment four storeys above the ground. Not bothering to lock his car doors, Edmund climbed the steps from the footpath to the glass-panelled timber doors but they were locked, as apartment building doors were. Beside the doors was a panel of poorly lit buttons marked with the numbers of every apartment in the building and some names of residents. An adjacent small speaker emitted a soft sound when Edmund's finger pressed the button for apartment 41, mimicking the louder buzzing in her home far above him. His finger pulled away and the sound stopped.

Every prior time he'd pressed that button, her eager voice emanated from the speaker. "Hi," she would address the person whose face she couldn't see. "Edmund?" she would check, from the privacy of her home, before pressing the button on her lounge room wall to allow him to open the building door.

The speaker remained silent. Edmund stared through the glass panels into the building, but no one entered the building foyer.

Her voice uttering his name every other time he'd been there had welcomed him more warmly than he'd realised. Having admitted him into the building, she normally waited for him in the open doorway of her intimate apartment, threw her arms around him when he reached her, and kissed him more passionately than he kissed her. If she was speaking on the telephone or preparing food in her kitchen then she would leave her apartment door slightly ajar and he would quietly push it open, go to her, and softly kiss her cheek, without interrupting her. They kissed each time they saw each other and every time they parted.

Edmund again pressed the button; his imagination heard the tone buzzing in her lounge room. He was ashamedly so ignoble as to hope she wasn't there, standing by the speaker, hiding from only him.

He pressed the button for apartment 42; its speaker emitting a soft tone. He pressed the next button and the next, pressing all the buttons for apartments on that floor. There were buttons marked for single people, pairs of people, and families. Most buttons were left blank for the privacy of residents. They might've been people who knew Candice or people Edmund passed in a corridor or stood with in a lift when he was visiting her home; they didn't need to know him. He would not ask anyone to admit him into the building, but ask somebody to tell him what had happened.

Edmund pressed more buttons and then more, pressing the buttons of all apartments on all the floors, running his finger over them in a punctuated melody demanding that somebody reply, metaphorically thumping every door in case somebody could hear. Buzzing tones in every lounge room might've been the only noises in the building, but they were a fervent orchestra from somebody wanting an audience to hear him.

6

FLEEING THE CITY

The thoughts he'd already made that day Edmund made again, of wars and storms and something somewhere to see; the empty city should never have ceased perplexing him since he first stepped outside that morning. No longer could he concoct the hope that more people were with him. He had no reason to remain.

Edmund drove uninterrupted to the nearest road leading out of the city centre, void of traffic but for him, the speed of his car accelerating. Fretting too much to care about traffic lights or speed limits and no longer imagining cars approaching him along cross streets of empty buildings at the edges of his vision, he barrelled onwards to wherever he was going: his chance to survive. The noise scattered birds. His wake scattered leaves.

Still eluding him was the reason he could live so much of a filling day without hearing another living voice or seeing another bewildered wanderer. Other solitary people might've found each other and fled in the fastest of their cars while he worked, or might be together in someone's home. The sky became larger in his sights, away from the tallest office and apartment buildings, without signs of a calamity.

The clear wide road rolled onwards, through precincts of old houses. A roadblock keeping cars away might soon appear ahead, beyond which might be a camping ground for evacuees. Places at which Edmund might find hordes of cowering people stumbled through his mind: sporting arenas, parade grounds. The day was a game he wanted to win by finding where everyone was hiding.

Edmund began to wonder if he could've done more to find people than he had done, that suddenly empty Tuesday. He hadn't seen the central railway station or most of the city streets. He hadn't gone to a hospital, surely part of the world still living. All Edmund knew ultimately was that he knew nothing of the almost empty city.

The road proceeded into suburbs of newer houses, rolling past. Edmund lifted himself higher in his driver's seat to see a little further ahead, but the people were not yet ready to appear. He sat back down and glanced at the rear-vision mirror and the empty road shrinking behind him. Street signs and directions identified places he'd never visited, while he remained on a main road driving outward.

Soft hills and fields of deepening green rose ahead of him beyond the city outskirts, without plumes of smoke or sight of people huddled there, clasping whatever suitcases they'd packed. The people who'd fled might've gone anywhere, in any direction. They were refugees from nothingness and from the fear of something else, who might return from the far side of town behind him while he fled towards the danger from which they'd escaped. The danger they'd eluded might be waiting there for him.

More than he feared dying by being the last man left, Edmund rued missing opportunity. If he knew which way to go, he'd drive to see the great event played live before him. There might be sightseers observing the city skyline or something else for spectacle. They'd sit on chairs they'd brought or stand. They'd eat picnic lunches and drink beverage they bought from vendors with vans, carts, and trays. Some would be there throughout, while others drifted in and out when the experience bored them. There'd be journalists interviewing them and commentating, some under spotlight before cameras. Other cameras would be filming the day and night in readiness for anything to see, compiling reams of documentary footage.

Witnesses would record their visions to retain, but mere images of news Edmund could see later, played back in countless bulletins and highlights. He had more reason to regret than he had cause to be afraid of what he didn't know.

Shining from a tall sign adjoining the road ahead of him was the familiar emblem of an oil company, below which were displayed the prices of varieties of petrol at a petrol station there. The gauge on his car dashboard meant the small light would soon glow, warning him the fuel tank was almost empty. Suddenly uncertain of his actions, Edmund let the speed of his car slow until it stopped, still in the middle of the road. Adjoining the petrol station, the lights inside a large supermarket also shone. The gentle engine continued to work, while Edmund sat in his stilled car.

His mobile telephone remained operative, but the screen confirmed he'd not missed any calls and listed no waiting messages. He dialled the number of his home and heard the tone ring enough times to know no messages were recorded there, without waiting to hear his recorded voice responding.

Nothing that day made sense to him, struck dumb by what had happened to the small universe in which he'd resided for so long, but Edmund baulked at travelling alone into so comprehensive an unknown. If the people of the city were hiding beyond the hills, ensconced in cars and makeshift homes until the danger times had passed, they mightn't have spare food for him to eat or excess petrol for his car. He might drive throughout the declining afternoon and evening but never find them. The largest petrol stations and supermarkets were open almost every day and night, and were as much a chance he would find somebody alive as was travelling alone into the countryside.

Parking his car at the supermarket entrance, beside two cars already there, a conversation he once shared with Candice slipped back into his memory. "One of my friends, when she was single," Candice had said, one night they ate dinner together, "met single men by going to a suburban supermarket late at night and loitering by the bananas."

"Did any of them become her husband?"

"Yes," she replied, "the supermarket night manager."

This was only afternoon, but the afternoon was getting late. The cooling open air enjoyed a slight consistent breeze, breaching the silence with a long murmur of nothing left to say.

Edmund dressed into his jacket over the rest of his suit, locked his car doors, and walked towards the plate glass doors between glass panels ready to meet someone. Sensors responded to anybody coming and the supermarket doors slid open.

Queues of trolleys, designed to veer towards the shelves, stood pushed together near him, inviting Edmund to take one. The long wide aisles shone brightly, reflecting the multitude of brash white fluorescent lights on the ceiling. Colourfully packaged foodstuffs and consumable homewares filled rows of waiting shelves.

The only checkout counters open included one with a sign denoting the maximum number of items customers could bring through that counter. Sometimes very late at night, few customers were in supermarkets, but at least one store employee always attended the self-service registers, ensuring customers passed the products bought across the bar-code scanners. That quiet afternoon, none was. The doors drew closed behind him.

No gentle music played, encouraging people to expend. The supermarket store was silent, but for the squeaking from Edmund's leather shoes walking in even steps across the vinyl floor. Somebody should hear the sounds his shoes emitted.

Edmund walked into the body of the supermarket and along the front of the long aisles, looking down them for anybody there. His pace quickened as he walked without seeing anyone, until he reached the last aisle and began running down that aisle to the far end of the supermarket, that running leather thumping on smooth vinyl. His suit wasn't tailored to be athletic and his jacket and long trousers cramped his shoulders and running limbs. At the end of that last aisle, Edmund stopped and looked along the back of the rows of shelves to the space of floor he couldn't have seen from the front of the supermarket. "Hello!" he called out. "Please talk to me."

He didn't move, for fear his footsteps on the floor prevented him from hearing anybody answer. Perhaps he ought to have felt foolish for running and calling out in such a public place. He would apologise to anybody complaining that he had.

Edmund walked slowly back along an aisle to the front of the supermarket, listening for nothing to hear beyond his footsteps on the floor. The time on clocks large and small was approaching five o'clock, Tuesday afternoon, but the senses of the city were frozen late on Monday night: a witching hour when everyone had gone away, without a summons or a warning he had heard.

A large noticeboard with glossy colour photographs of the employees in smiling portraiture dominated a wall. They could've been missing people notices like those in the police station, although they were only the people missing from one silent supermarket. Those boards could've properly displayed photographs of all the people in the world.

Nothing there could tell Edmund where the people might've gone. Several deliberately conspicuous security cameras hovered from the ceiling, surveying the aisles and counters for people attempting to steal goods from the store. The supermarket presumably employed a guard to sit in a hidden room and watch television monitors on which were playing the images the cameras recorded. Edmund stood where a pervasive camera pointed directly at him and looked up into the lens. The guard mightn't have heard Edmund calling out but couldn't avoid seeing him, the only person in the store, staring back at him.

The supermarket remained silent. The guard didn't take the microphone to talk to him through the public address loudspeakers or leave his desk to go to him. Edmund waved at him, unable to see whether the guard waved back. Waving didn't move the guard to do more than standing there had done. The guard wasn't there to talk to strangers but to identify thieves and other wrongdoers. Edmund needed to be a thief.

He looked back at the shelves of merchandise and thought of

things to take. The cold storage refrigerators provided Edmund with a clear plastic packet of smoked salmon slices and plastic cartons of strawberry skim milk yoghurt. Biscuits in the office and his small breakfast hadn't been enough to eat that day.

Edmund walked back to the registers carrying that food, suddenly uncertain what to do. He could pay for what he bought at a self-serve register, but a security guard watching him wouldn't know to tell him where everybody was. Edmund didn't want the stigma of being arrested for shoplifting, but he needed a reason for the security guard to talk with him.

He took his wallet from his pocket and, leaving his notes of cash and coins insides it, removed one of his gold plastic credit cards. The card would be his answer to any charge for theft if somebody arrested him, and he stood it atop the register in full view of the camera, recording him. "I want to make a purchase," he called out, to avoid being accused of doing what he was doing.

Nobody came. No voices emanated from loudspeakers in the store. Edmund passed the striped barcode of the salmon packet over the scanner, as a customer would do. The item and sale price registered. He did the same thing with the yoghurt carton, without concluding the transaction and inserting or sliding his credit card with its electronic chip and stripe as he ought to have done. The register's electronic display showed him how much money he wasn't paying.

Confident he could defend himself from accusation of theft, but not ignorance, Edmund proceeded slowly past the register, where the store only permitted people who'd paid for their goods to go. Edmund reached across the customer service counter and took a small white plastic spoon, complimentary when a person bought yoghurt.

Carrying his food and spoon, Edmund walked slowly across the floor to the glass doors and world outside. He listened for the sounds of somebody hurrying through the store towards him, but the only sounds beyond his footsteps were those of the glass doors opening automatically for him.

Still inside the supermarket, Edmund stopped and turned around. Nobody was coming to apprehend him.

Edmund was not a thief until he left the store, but he would finish what he'd started. He turned back to the open doors and walked through them. The doors slid closed behind him.

The murmurings of the little breeze became louder each time he heard them anew. Edmund stood alone in the clear air. The car park might've been the same property as was the supermarket, but a security guard could call him a thief and detain him.

The guard might've needed more time to get from his desk through the store to reach the perpetrator of the crime. He might've been away from his room when Edmund was at the register, but returned to see the monitor as the criminal escaped from the store.

Edmund waited for the guard, but the glass doors remained closed. No one appeared beyond them. A solitary guard would need to leave the supermarket unattended if he went into the car park and so might remain sitting at his desk. Edmund resumed walking the short distance to his car.

No footsteps sounded but those he made. Edmund left his acquisitions on the front passenger seat of his car, closed and locked the door, and hurried back through the wide open supermarket doors. He again stood before the silent security camera, waving his arms high in the air to attract attention from anybody watching the monitor or within casual eyeshot of it. "I'm here," he called out, waving his arms enough for the momentum through his shoulders almost to lift him from the floor. "Talk to me."

Nothing happened. Nobody responded loud enough for him to hear. Edmund's arms soon became sore and he dropped them to his side. His voice dipped to speak a final retreating utterance: "I'm here."

The supermarket surrounded him, with its clean white space of aisles and glut of food and wares. The manager or another person had left it insecure, but Edmund might've been the only person to take anything: two perishable small items and a spoon.

Edmund took a shopping trolley, pushed it along the aisles and every shelf of items his solitude afforded him, his momentary fortune, and collected an abundance of food and beverage he normally bought in minor quantities. A sealed packet of sliced tender beef appealed, but the sticks of bread were no longer fresh; someone ought to have known better than leaving them in dispensing trays. Replacement light globes for his apartment, bottles of shampoo, and toiletries for hygiene were always useful. Powders for his dishwashing and clothes washing machines would eventually be used. Black polish would clean his leather shoes.

Venturing into the finest imported and local fare, he couldn't find any truffles. Tin cans of little fish, fragile small sardines, were novel foods.

Edmund continued until he couldn't slip or squeeze any more packets, bags, and bottles into the trolley, almost overflowing with the bounty for which he would gladly pay if necessity required. The trolley wheels struggled against the vinyl under casters, as he forced the trolley towards the self-serve register, still listing his salmon and yoghurt. He wouldn't need to visit a supermarket again for weeks.

"Hello," he called again, in a precautionary measure not expecting any answer. Edmund again tapped his credit card atop the register, more briefly this time. "I want to buy some things."

Ticking through his mind, time enough for his excuse had passed. Edmund thought of leaving the store immediately, pushing the trolley to his car, but he had no cause to hurry. In his charade before the camera, he collected a second trolley. He removed each item he would've bought from the first, passed its barcode across the scanner, cumulating the items he was taking and the purported price of them, and placed it in a plastic bag from the dispensing rack: heavier items first, like items together. He stowed the filled bags in the second trolley, as customers would do. Subtly, so the camera would not detect it, he hastened the pace at which he worked to leave before anyone returned.

In a last defence before departing, he held his credit card in the air. "Hello," he called again, pretending. Edmund wanted the person he saw to be someone outside the store who would not care what he had done. He pushed the trolley away from the counter, through the opening glass doors, to the car park.

The muted sun had slipped too far still to cast shadows. The murmur of the streets had become a little louder. The breeze escorted fallen leaves dancing across the ground.

Listening for the sounds of anybody watching him, Edmund opened his car boot and lifted the plastic bags of shopping into it. He left the trolley near his car, knowing a person's job was to return trolleys to the store.

The supermarket had provided him with all he needed and some of what he wanted, but had provided nothing for his car. No cars stood by any bowsers at the petrol station although one was parked outside the glass walls of the apparently empty store and cashier's desk, from which electric lights shone unperturbed. Edmund parked his car at the bowser nearest the entrance to the store.

The glass doors to the petrol station store opened as he approached them, as they'd done at the supermarket. "Hello," Edmund called out, resuming his performance for the sake of more security cameras and recordings. "Hello." Television monitors at the cashier's empty desk broadcast images from cameras in the shop and near the bowsers, but the only person Edmund saw broadcast on the screens was he, looking across the desk at an image of him doing so. Cameras watched and never noticed him.

Edmund returned to his car, where he flicked the switch on the floor beside the driver's seat to release the cover to the cap on the petrol tank. He unscrewed the cap and let it hang by its short cord, in the routine of other days. The electronic displays on the bowser panel identified the amount and cost of fuel taken by the last customer at that pump, whenever he or she was there. Edmund lifted the premium petrol handset from its bowser mount and those numbers flickered back to zero, before he pushed the handset nozzle into the closely fitting opening to his petrol tank and pressed the handset lever.

He stood waiting for the car to fill, just as he'd stood many times at other stations all the same, while the sounds of clicking meters marked the petrol gushing to his car. No price was more pervasive than the price of petrol, displayed so ubiquitously and so frequently called upon, but the price was suddenly unimportant.

Everything seemed normal in the small space around him, where a person pumping petrol into a car could be standing there alone. In a custom of his life unchanged, the day was again ordinary. The moment could've been one from any greying late afternoon. The familiarity assured him he needn't be afraid.

The petrol stopped flowing when the tank was nearly full. Edmund flexed his fingers on the lever to eject more petrol into the tank until it began overflowing. Much of his fear aroused by an empty city had abated in the shelves of a well-stocked supermarket and tanks of a surplus petrol station. Habitually trying not to spill fuel drops on his car or the ground, Edmund returned the handset to the bowser, sealed the cap back on his car, and replaced the cover.

Edmund could've swiped his credit card across a sensor at the pump to pay for the petrol he had taken, but he walked back into the shop as most customers did. He took some chocolates from the trays along the front of the cashier's desk, waved his credit card where the cameras saw it, and departed.

7

THE FLICKERING LIGHT

Through the settling dusk of day, Edmund looked for hints of anyone about. No more cars were parked in sight, although houses had private garages that would conceal them.

The suburban streets and homes around him were still. Perhaps they always were, with too few people to be called crowds and too few cars to be called traffic. People strolling along paths didn't make the noise they made hurrying through city malls, although birds in trees and the sporadic barking of a dog made the suburbs noisier than the city had been that day.

Only birds wanting daylight flew in the air. The sun shone brighter in the late-day sky than in the shadowed streets below it.

Beyond the suburbs with their subdued light of evening was empty countryside, so far as Edmund could discern. It didn't stir with sounds that reached him by his car. If animals were in the fields then they rested where Edmund couldn't see them. They might've been sleeping in the forests where anything could hide. He could see too few houses, sheltered in the greenery, to accommodate the people who had fled. The encroaching night made greenery a grey becoming black.

Edmund might've been the only person to know that he was

there, gazing awkwardly at twilight and the world. His mind had seen sufficient reason to be afraid, but he couldn't feel a fear.

Street lights, spread more sparsely through the suburbs than in the city centre, flickered alight, according to the times and lights that controllers had programmed them to shine. The lights of late-night business premises remained bright around Edmund and his car, but no lights shone from any houses.

Breaking the stillness of the scenery around him, among the last dark suburban houses, a light flickered in a window. The early evening made the single light more noticeable than it would otherwise have been, but lights normally ignited because somebody started them. Houses had doors on which Edmund could knock and windows he could reach, unlike most apartments. He started to walk towards that small enticing light.

The house beckoning him was much like any tranquil house around it, if slightly smaller in façade. The light shone from a wide glass window, across which hung curtains thick enough to conceal everything but the light. No tall furniture or person shaded the curtains lit beyond it, so far as Edmund could yet see. Walking increasingly more rapidly, he reached the street, crossed it without looking for traffic, and rushed up to the closed front door.

Edmund pressed the button by the solid wooden door, whereby an electric bell rang inside. He knocked his fingers hard against the door, without glass panels or peepholes through which he could peer at shadows coming to him, before listening for the sounds of someone coming to assist. That person would be a stranger with whom he had no reputation to embarrass; Edmund needed only to ask about the news without concern for what the stranger thought.

Nobody came. Edmund stepped away from the door and peeked through the edges of the window around the curtains towards the hiding light. The top of a sofa was visible to him, but not anyone in the room. He again pressed the button by the door and heard again the sound of the electric bell ringing in the house.

Edmund walked along the ground outside the window for

every glimpse that he could get inside the room in which the light was shining: part of a drab wall led to the tarnished frame of a dark painting. A window without steel bars across it was probably wired to an alarm; Edmund had no reason to smash the glass.

He again pressed the button, heard the bell ring inside the house, and knocked his fingers on the door, but he'd stopped believing that anyone would answer. People wanting to ward off burglars by making their home seem occupied and people not wanting to come home to lonely darkness set their lights to shine automatically late afternoon. An electric timer igniting the light would later switch it off again, as it did every day and night. "Damn," said Edmund, striking the side of his frustrated fist hard against the door.

"Go away," cried out an angry voice.

Edmund quickly turned back to face it, from the far side of the door. "Hello," he said.

"Go away." The voice was a woman's voice.

"I need to talk with you."

"Go away."

"Please, I need to talk with you. It's important."

"I am not going anywhere," insisted the voice. "I said last night I'm not going anywhere, and I'm still not going."

"I want to ask you a question."

The house beyond the door was again silent, while Edmund listened for any sound the woman made. "Are you with the police?" she asked.

"No."

"Why should I answer your question?"

"If you don't, I'll knock on your door all night."

The woman Edmund couldn't see was again silent, presumably contemplating how best to deal with his intrusion. Finally, a small electric light flickered and shone over his head, illuminating him. The round door handle slowly turned. The door slowly opened.

A metal chain from the door into a slot in the doorframe prevented the door from opening more than a few inches. The creases in her skin obscured some of the marks that time had sprinkled on the woman's elderly stern face, crouched behind the door. "What is your question?" she asked.

"Where is everyone?"

"What?"

"You know that everyone has gone," said Edmund.

"Of course, I know that everyone has gone," she told him. "That doesn't mean I have to go."

"Do you know where they went?"

"No."

"Do you know why they left?"

"No."

"Don't you care that they've gone?" asked Edmund.

"They can go whatever they like. That doesn't mean I have to go." The actions of other people weren't sufficient reason for anyone to act.

"Can you tell me what happened last night?"

"You're asking too many questions."

"I won't be much longer."

"Mister Cusack," she grumbled, "came knocking on my door, much in the way you did, and told me we all had to go. I told him that I have lived in this house for sixty-eight years and I wasn't going to leave it now. He argued about it, until I slammed the door in his face and he left me alone."

"Did he tell you why you had to leave?"

"No."

"Was there anything on the television or radio?"

"People know I don't have time for frivolities," she said, as if Edmund should've known.

"Did Mister Cusack say there was a warning of some kind?" asked Edmund.

"I wasn't listening."

"Are we in danger?"

"People make warnings about everything," she said, "but nothing ever comes of them. People get all excited about this or that, but I'm not leaving my perfectly good house to follow some fool warning. I didn't leave last night, I'm not leaving tonight, and I'm not leaving tomorrow night either. When they all come back and see that nothing came of all their warnings then we'll see what they have to say about me, but tonight I'm staying in my nice home, thank you very much. There, are you happy now?"

Edmund didn't know his answer to her question. He'd learned the solution to the paradox was orderly and rational, without knowing what it was. "One more thing," he said.

"Yes," she sighed.

"Do you shop at the supermarket over there?" His head tilted towards the bright store lights. "The specials are very good tonight."

She closed the door and shook it in its lock, fortifying her home. She extinguished the light above him.

"Thank you," Edmund called out. "Good night."

No other house lights shone. People might've been scattered among the silent houses and apartments throughout the city and might've even seen him, but they needn't bother Edmund if he didn't bother them. The cantankerous old woman made the motives of people leaving less important than the fact they ran away. He wouldn't waste time searching for people who weren't there.

The warning of calamity might've reached everyone but him, but the day was over and no calamity transpired; no human wars had come or natural disasters struck. He was ready to escape at any sign of looming tragedy, but he hadn't seen or heard a sign. The longer Edmund remained in the city without incident, the less reason he had for leaving. His telephone might yet ring with the voice of someone telling him to flee, but he wouldn't run until it did. Like the old woman reclusive in her home, he'd survived that day within the city and the suburbs and would survive another.

If people fled because of fear, they'd been wrong to leave. They weren't about to die.

If Edmund was too complacent then all of them had been complacent before that Monday night. He might've been the optimist, but optimism was a quality without which he never could've coped.

His life was secure in the city, and he might never find again the amenities he enjoyed if he left them far behind. Whatever sun, wind, or hydroelectric schemes of falling water powered the grids of wires, electricity would come as long as the sun shone, wind blew, or water flowed down mountains. Whatever coal, gas, or oil burnt continued to burn. The powers of automation would pump water through the pipes into the taps of homes and offices. They didn't need people to operate them every day.

The empty night of country remained dark, but for the last lights above the road reaching into it and too few stars to guide him. The camps or cars or other receptacles in which the hordes were huddled were no place to be when his soft bed waited for him at his apartment. He wouldn't go somewhere strange to be alone, uninterested, and cold, or expend his days wandering from idle solitude to the next. He might drive forever and not find them, while they returned from their needless sanctuary to their safe city and suburban beds. The hordes might return that night, and dress for work and shopping in the morning as they did on any Wednesday morning.

The danger in which the old woman did not believe had surely passed. Whatever was happening to the world, Edmund couldn't do anything about it. Everything would soon return to being what it had been, the good times coming back.

Surrendering his mind and thoughts, Edmund removed his jacket and hung it from a hook inside his car. The time on the dashboard clock was six o'clock, an hour before the time he'd proposed to Candice that they meet. Descartes' restaurant, like every other restaurant, was surely closed, but his best chance to see her was to be where she could find him. He had no reason to be anywhere but there.

Driving slower than he could've driven, Edmund drove his car out of the petrol station, pausing more from practice than intuition before the red shining traffic light. The sensors under the road recorded the presence of his car, while he looked around for a camera that would record him violating traffic laws if he drove onwards. He couldn't wave a credit card outside the window of his car as he could've waved one in the supermarket and petrol station, and the absence of other cars was no excuse for driving past red traffic lights.

The lights became green. Edmund calmly drove onto the main

road back to the city centre, on the far side of the road along which he'd fled in his anxiety that afternoon.

The radio played recorded music and advertisements to which Edmund listened, as he normally listened driving alone. Traffic lights facing him remained green, without vehicles approaching from lesser roads that would've made lights red to defy him. Intermittently he glanced at the rear-vision mirror or at the buildings by which he passed, and never saw a moving light except his own reflected in the glass, sliding smoothly through the streets.

Ahead of him, reaching high above the road and houses and among the sky for stars, were the neon fluorescent lights of the city centre. Lights plied in shops and office buildings in the random patterns that people had set them alight on prior days or to shine automatically each night: the automatic land they left behind. Birds and other strangers outside the buildings couldn't see into the stone and silver catacombs by day, but the lights left shining from the ceilings exposed people without shadows sitting at their desks each evening. The shining floors of offices were a myriad of shelves of silver ornaments at night, when the bright and darkened window squares hung in the air.

The scene of city buildings could've been any evening, but without the little people sitting at their desks and with the cleaners suddenly excused. The lights brightened the floors for people who had fled, while Edmund remained to see what endured inside the city space. He hadn't seen the lights when he was working in them, except perhaps on nights he worked too late and for a moment paused to look outside his office window and want a place to rest. The stillness where activity had been could've left the skyline hollow, but the lights at night made the city resilient and strong. The city from a distance was impervious to the fears that had driven people from it.

The people he would ordinarily have seen had left, but not told Edmund they were leaving. The concert to which Candice had had two tickets on Monday evening might never have occurred, or might've been underway when somebody at the conservatorium announced that everyone should leave. Announcements might've occurred across the city, while

Edmund languished at his desk earning money oblivious to them. Private conversations informed old women in their homes too obstinate to heed them, but nobody knocked on his apartment door or pressed the communication button beside the building door, unless he was at his office when someone did. The city had stopped revolving while he worked.

Hugh Garrett could've told him, except he wanted Edmund at his desk until he finished drafting the submission. Garrett might've left his home before Edmund sent it. The relationships between employees were avowedly professional and impersonal; their responsibilities didn't require them to save each other's lives.

The taxi driver Monday night could've told Edmund if the news he offered to disclose had been important, whatever else he thought about the passenger in the paying seat behind him. Nobody telephoned Edmund through Monday night, unless he was too tired to hear the ringing. His friends had been merely business networking in their mutually exclusive careers.

More than any other person, Edmund would've expected Candice to contact him Monday evening, however much he'd distressed or angered her. If she'd vowed never again to see him, then would a warning to evacuate the city have made her renege upon that vow? She mightn't have known he was alone in his office, or might've assumed that people wanting work from him that night had spoken to him. She might've assumed that other people he'd referred to as his friends would contact him, but he'd seen too little of them in recent years. Every moral compunction in her commanded that Candice wouldn't let him die, but he wasn't about to die.

The changing colours of traffic lights, from red to green and back to orange and to red after he passed, weren't important anymore, even if cameras photographed him breaching them. The police weren't there to withdraw his driver licence. In a city of regulation, he was the individual unregulated.

No car would collide with his, although Edmund's feet were poised to brake. Sometimes he glanced along a side street to see whether another car approached, uncertain whether he wanted one to be there. His car lights streaming along the street remained estranged from every light they passed. Edmund didn't bother imagining the words to say to anyone he met.

Edmund was surely not unique. He might merely have been the most misfortunate during the twenty-four past hours. He might also have become the most fortunate, to come to be alone in a city without danger. His abject solitude mightn't have been the loneliness of a person banished from the group. It might've also been the quiet seclusion of a man who'd chosen not to go.

The city functioned without people in it and could do so long after everyone had gone. Edmund didn't know whether to laugh that it was unconcerned by people not working for a day, or to cry that it could carry on without them in their careers. Working people might've done enough to become redundant and redundancy at work was better than they'd realised it would be. The submission he'd drafted late Monday night and the work he'd done that morning were blips in a time capsule that hadn't changed a thing.

Factories could continue producing widgets from assembly lines no one remained to want. Inventories for no one left to buy them would clog the output trays; accumulating assets in their idolatry before which no one remained to kneel. Their perpetual production might be a great achievement of which his people would be proud, when next they thought about them, or they might just have been the things that people did. In his career and conversations, Edmund had often talked and written about robotics and mechanical arms and brains, but never seen them. Days of commerce and occupation had been lost among the patterns of office cubicles and meeting rooms.

Edmund's car slowed as it entered the grid of central city streets, where the lights of the silent city were brightest and most densely set. Their reflections echoed in the glass and steel, multiplying them many-fold and blaring over Edmund in his car, but the streets remained as empty under electric lights as they'd been under sunlight through the day.

He stopped his car in the centre of the street, before the building in which he worked. The offices were dark.

At the corner of the floor, Hugh Garrett's office enjoyed more windows than Edmund's did. Edmund imagined the old man standing at the glass, where he'd often seen him standing. "I love this city," Garrett standing there once told him, talking as much about himself, "this crystal manor." Garrett paused, as he did when he wanted the words and ideas that echoed around his office every day to permeate another person's mind. "You must want to be what I am. You must want to have a job like mine, car like mine, office like mine." His large hands, with their palms wide open, rested against the glass. "You must want a house like mine, and it is a marvellous house."

Edmund hadn't seen the older man's home, but didn't doubt that it was marvellous. He wouldn't have called his apartment marvellous; he wouldn't have called anything that he possessed marvellous.

"When you become what I am and have what I have," Garrett continued, "then you must continue to want to be and have more. Clawing at the heels of your handcrafted shoes will be men and women like you now, who will want to be what you are and to have what you have. They'll wrench you and yours from you, if they can."

Edmund couldn't help but earn more money as he worked, but if company results ever began to falter, critics would call resolve obstinacy and experience inertia. Eventually, they'd compel a person to spend each day in the house he or she might call marvellous.

The night was early, but Edmund wouldn't return to his office where Candice from the street might see lights above his desk. Besides, he needn't return there to know the trays on his desk contained no incoming correspondence. The rubbish he'd dropped in the bins late Monday night and Tuesday was still there. Lying undisturbed on his desk was the thick submission he'd sent to people who didn't like each other and who didn't think enough about him to like or dislike him. All his work might do was increase the dividends paid to already wealthy shareholders, reduce the prices of the company's products paid by customers already able to afford them, and add to the year-end bonus the company paid Hugh Garrett.

The pretence that once shrouded his vocation had evaporated into night. Edmund would work when his mind had mood to exercise and leave the office at his whim. If anyone snapped at his heels then Edmund didn't notice. If office building windows reaching high above him made Garrett appear small, then Edmund was even smaller: two little faces in the glass.

8

A HUMMINGBIRD IN AN ACORN FARM

Lights shone from some shops and restaurants but not from Descartes' restaurant, tucked away since Monday night. Without regard for signs about legal and illegal parking, Edmund parked at the kerb outside it. He would've driven onto the footpath, but didn't want to damage his car.

Everything was silent, as it had always been. Street lights illuminated the empty tables by the window of the otherwise dark restaurant, awaiting customers not coming. The chefs, waiters, and waitresses dressed in their black and white uniforms, who dispensed meals each lunch and dinner time, hadn't come to work that day.

The first time Edmund ate there, as a guest of Hugh Garrett, Edmund stared in awe at the manicured entree laid before him. Two wine glasses towered over it: one for the introductory white and the other for the red to accompany the main course coming. A corporate account made appetites and taste buds blossom. During the years following, Edmund drank wine from bottles becoming older in restaurants becoming newer. Without noticing each step in the extravagance that had become familiar in his life, they dulled his senses before the hours he expended at the office disheartened him.

If his success imprisoned him then it was because Edmund

couldn't live without expense. He became dependant on luxuries before he became unable to enjoy them; he couldn't live less well than he'd grown accustomed to living.

The last time Edmund and Candice ate in Descartes', he had been working late. He raced along the footpath and bounded into the restaurant, when she clapped her hands in mock applause. A waiter smiled and clapped with her, as did a group laughing at his expense. "I'm sorry I'm late," he told her, before kissing her lips and the taste of the aperitif she'd almost finished drinking. "I couldn't get away."

Sitting alone in his car, Edmund smiled to think again about that night. The tiramisu had been exquisite, although the waiter brought his brandy at room temperature instead of serving it in a warm glass.

The radio advertised another restaurant; chairs in restaurants where once Edmund queued to get a table were empty. The radio would play recorded music and advertisements all night if Edmund let it. He switched it off.

A different night alone, in the silent darkness of his car, he might've imagined a thief trying to open the door beside him, brandishing a gun or knife and demanding to have his wallet. Edmund watched the shadows of the footpath and building entranceways for any menace lurking there, but saw nothing to fear. Without a danger left to face, he was comfortable being the only person there.

The streets of lights at night remained empty, as the time drifted past seven o'clock. Lying on the passenger seat beside him were the first items he'd taken from the supermarket, which would spoil if they remained too long a period without refrigeration. Edmund opened the packet of salmon and ate it with his fingers. He opened the carton of fruit yoghurt and used his plastic spoon to place small portions in his mouth, affording Candice more minutes to arrive. When Edmund finished, he cleaned the spoon with his lips and tongue and stowed it in the pocket in the door.

The night was a chance to play, and Edmund tried to think of things to do. A conversation might interest him, but he could speak only with his reflection. There could be no parties in anybody's home without anybody there.

Activities apart from work he could undertake unaccompanied didn't fall readily to mind. The night was like the worst of public holidays with every entertainment closed. He couldn't enjoy a sporting contest or see a play in a theatre. He couldn't visit a gallery or museum. For all his money, he couldn't buy amusement. He couldn't amuse himself by leisure left alone.

Edmund ambled to the door of Descartes' restaurant, a step above the footpath. As best as he could see, no security cameras hung from the high corners of the walls. Edmund didn't need to eat anymore or drink but would say that he was hungry or thirsty to anybody apprehending him, or later learning what he'd done. He pushed the closed doors at their locks.

Nobody called out to stop him. The locks remained fast.

He pushed harder, trying not to break the doors or make a noise. The doors quivered, resisting him and holding the lock together. Edmund pushed the doors again, contemplating how much he had lawful excuse to do. He was the law-conforming citizen playing the amateur, unlicensed rogue. Adrenaline rushed within him as a door slipped from its fittings and opened.

His arms and hands stopped although his heart continued racing, seeing what he'd done. He looked back at the street. The restaurant was open just for him and his patronage, because of him and his bare hands. No police sirens wailed to draw anyone towards him.

Slowly his heart settled without anyone to stoke it, while he became the new intruder. He was the figure in silhouette before the confined space of darkness until, pushing the doors wide open, the light coming from the street behind him lifted some shades of black to shades of grey. He switched on the soft ceiling lights, in the restaurant open for only him.

The tables were bare, cleared away since diners last ate there. Pushed under them were complementing chairs. Somebody might've cleaned the carpet, or perhaps those diners and their waiters never dropped anything.

Edmund didn't need to wait or let anyone ahead of him, but

the maître d' was not at his wooden lectern to welcome him. Edmund walked around it to check the reservations book, beneath a long brass light. Beside the book lay an eraser with three pencils; reservations were marked in pencil because patrons changed and failed to honour them.

The book was open at the pages for Monday past. Edmund turned over a page, to Tuesday. The Schultz party of four had been due at six and the Seveque party of two at six thirty. Edmund glanced at the watch on his wrist; the restaurant only allowed patrons fifteen minutes grace before they surrendered their reservations. Edmund erased those entries. He could've demanded his usual table without a reservation but instead he wrote "*7 pm Neale 2.*" The time was his to be there, and he added a note: "*– no sharing.*"

"Thank you," said Edmund, leaving some money as a tip.

Several leather-bound menu covers stood in a rectangular compartment in the lectern. The lamb was most inviting, but not the liver pâté. Most guests chose desserts after they'd eaten their main courses. The restaurant accepted all major credit cards and the kitchen closed at ten o'clock that evening.

Normally a setting for chefs but invisible to patrons, the kitchen was open to his inspection. Aboard trolleys inside the kitchen door were piles of neatly folded clean white tablecloths and napkins, along with small buckets of silver clean cutlery standing upright. Clear crystal glasses and porcelain crockery stood on the high shelves on a wall and two brass corkscrews lay on a table. Edmund touched everything he wanted to touch, without a chef telling him he could not.

Edmund couldn't cook the ingredients to make too complicated a meal, but the refrigerator contained the last declining food of which paying patrons and restaurant staff had not availed themselves on Monday evening. The food that had been fresh would soon not be, although some wings and breast of duck smelt fresh enough to eat; they'd be more fulfilling than anything Edmund cooked in a vacant office kitchen. If he didn't eat them, then they never needed to have been made.

He set them on a plate he placed with a jug of sauce in a

microwave oven. He would mention to the maître d' his disappointment his meal was being reheated.

Near the kitchen door was a steep flight of stairs setting downwards. Activating a light above the stairs revealed a closed door below them, to which Edmund stepped. The door opened to darkness and cold air, until Edmund flicked a light switch on the wall. Scores of dusty wine bottles lay in tall racks between short corridors; the province of connoisseurs and their beneficiaries was Edmund's personal collection. The old uneven ground pressed the soles of his work shoes, while he perused the labels marked by aging years and the vintage names and crests.

Edmund wanted whatever vintage wine was most expensive, knowing little more about it, but the wine list with prices was upstairs. Dust crumbled in his fingers as he took a cool bottle of Gevrey-Chambertin in his hand, examined the motifs on the label and the year the grapes were harvested, and approved. The sealed cellar preserved the rest of Edmund's wine, to take and drink in the fullness of his time.

People returning to the city would know Edmund had remained, without requiring camera recordings. Anybody wanting his fingerprints as a memento of him being there could have them. In his worst scenario, he might pay for anything he took, but no judge would gaol him for seeming to be the only person left alive, an innocent mistake. A jury of his returning peers would envy him for what he did while they'd been away.

At a table by the window, Edmund set a single white cloth and two napkins: his dining room and picnic area. Two knives, forks, and little spoons along with two glasses were his setting made for two, shining in the light cast for them. In the kitchen, Edmund served the steaming duck on two plates, on which he poured hot sauce. He set the meals at his table as an obsequious waiter would've set it.

Edmund sat in the chair from which he looked up through the restaurant window towards his office window. Out of sight, Candice's face unchanged in photograph smiled innocently. He kissed the air and blew that kiss towards her, knowing the kiss couldn't make her smile any more or less than she already smiled. She wouldn't mind him starting his meal for one without her.

The restaurant was unduly large. Edmund savoured his rich meal more than he'd savoured foods he'd paid to eat, letting every taste and texture languish on his tongue and in his mouth and senses. When he finished eating, he sat sideways against the backrest and stretched out his long legs, without concern for waiters or patrons stepping over them, drinking solitary wine from his lazy, rested hand. Fresh meals might be all he missed, until the chefs returned.

If Candice had anything to say to him, then she wasn't coming there to say it. They'd shared some time and little more, and she might already be imagining the man who could share more with her than Edmund could.

Retired for the day, the choice was difficult between cognacs. Edmund chose the Camus. Without a tulip-shaped glass, he took a Napoleonic brandy glass he didn't know how to warm, but he poured the deep gold liquor until it filled the widest reaches of the glass. He then poured a little more.

Edmund gazed into the living fluid, his companion for the night. With its stem between his middle fingers and cradling the round glass in his palm, as Napoleon held Josephine's breast and nipple, he swirled the liquor in a circle, swelling it to the sides and letting it slide back in a slow dance to the heavens. His nose above it swept up the senses of the grapes as if he'd never before sensed them, before gently tilting the fortified breath of potency into his mouth, trapping it against his palate from which it would never leave.

When Edmund finished, tap water in the kitchen rinsed his empty glasses. He stood them upside down to dry, like a bartender at work or man at home. The dishwasher was full and he left his plate and cutlery in the sink, remembering the adage about customers unable to pay for their meals cleaning dishes in the kitchen. He could afford to smile. He could afford everything.

Edmund sealed the cork back in the wine bottle neck and returned the cognac bottle to other bottles, for his next visit to his private eating-house. He would leave other restaurants until he paid to eat there and not worry if he never did.

He retrieved his money from the maître d's lectern. The service had been very poor that night.

Edmund pulled closed the door and left. Candice's meal and wine remained on the table.

Street lights were gentle company while Edmund wandered in the cold, recalling times and places he couldn't safely walk at night. He walked where he wanted to walk, indifferent to the kerbs, the road a promenade for only him.

Being alone was an opportunity Edmund didn't comprehend, before society returned to constrain him back to earth. His time alone, with all that remained for him, was an experience to relish, although he wondered for how long his paradise would last. He wouldn't listen for the sounds of people coming back in case he heard them; police or soldiers would probably return before the fleets of people. The cause of people leaving shouldn't end before he'd done what he could only do without them. The world shouldn't return to him too soon.

Lights shone from a closed cafeteria, in which several closed umbrellas advertising brands of coffee leant against a wall and several small round tables and chairs stood stacked upon each other. Lying on a board and trestle were day-old newspapers and older magazines, which patrons were free to borrow while they waited, drank, and ate. They were the news of Monday morning and other ancient days, which had not foretold the days since then. Somebody else could read them.

Near a shining stainless steel-cloaked machine for making steam, frothing milk, and brewing coffee were bowls for *Café au Lait* and tall glasses for *Caffe Latte*. An empty grinder stood by bags of coffee beans and jars of ground coffee, with labels boasting everything inside them. Most claimed to be of European flavour better to taste. Edmund didn't think coffee plantations were in Europe.

He wouldn't try to do too much, but would take what he could take and not long for what he couldn't. A photographic store enclosed the most modern cameras. Nothing Edmund photographed would change.

The keepers of a jewellery store had packed their golden watches and diamond rings into safes on Monday night. Ornaments nobody touched or saw were meaningless, hidden in the dark security of iron tombs until someone set them free. Like the cash and other commodities filling impenetrable vaults within the finance houses, Edmund had no need to care about places he couldn't breach.

Adorning the side of another building were several large glass cases, in which hung posters of films showing and purportedly soon coming. Faces reached forward in dramatic poses of passion and power, adventure and experience, enticing passers-by into lives unlike their own. Film lives were equally unlike the life that Edmund's had become, except perhaps the life in the poster without people, but with a hummingbird hovering above an acorn farm. Edmund hadn't listened well enough to recall Candice's review of *Millstone Vanquished*.

The doors to the cinemas were locked. Edmund cursorily thumped a door. It snapped open, pounding against the wall inside the building and flopping back, in the adventure of his experience. He needed only a brief excuse for the small chance that anyone detained him and would quickly conceive it if that anyone appeared.

In the half-light from the street he found and pressed a switch on a wall igniting electric lights ahead of him. The cinema foyer was another space he saw serene for the first time. The sign above the booth selling tickets listed the films from the close of business Monday night, the last being *Millstone Vanquished*, but had not been set for the scheduled session times on Tuesday.

Tuesday was the day for cheap cinema tickets. From the racks behind the kiosk counter, Edmund took a plastic bag of toffee chocolates.

An usher had left the cinema doors open, through which Edmund passed. At the front of the cinema stood a tall, wide screen, facing rising rows of cushioned chairs. High in the black wall behind them were several small square windows.

Edmund walked up an aisle of stairs to dark curtains, pulled them aside, and saw a single door. It opened into a small projector room, lit only by the light that came through the small square windows. Pointing through one window was a large projector. A small exit light shone above a second door, through which the projectionist, having initiated a performance, could leave. Any person confined within their hidden space would see the same repeating film, starting again soon after it last finished.

A switch on the wall near him ignited a light in the centre of the room, revealing a large unsightly chair with fading brown upholstery. Along a wall were several shelves, on which lay half a dozen metal canisters to which were affixed adhesive stickers with film names printed on them and newer metal boxes, along with scores of well-read books and torn magazines. Edmund could see films on television sets at any time, but he'd never sat in a cinema playing a motion picture just for him: actors and actresses performing just for him.

He flicked the switch bringing the projector's lights to life. Uncertain what to do, he pressed another button and then another, when studio motifs shone across the distant screen and the studio signature melody began to play. Hurriedly, Edmund stood up from the chair, extinguished the lights in the small room, and rushed back into the cinema. The bright lights shining from the ceiling compromised the contrasts in the moving images, until he found a switch by the door to extinguish them, leaving the light reflected from the screen to dominate the auditorium for accompanying words and music. The movie light cast moving shadows on Edmund as he walked between the rows of seats in the centre of the cinema and sat where he wanted.

Relieved not to have arrived so late as to miss the movie's start, Edmund opened his packet of chocolates, unwrapped one, and placed it in his mouth. He replaced the empty wrapper in the bag. The moving images played on the screen and sounds of the story bellowed from speakers surrounding him.

His seat held him reclining back, stretching his free arm along the top of the seat beside him as men sitting alone could do. He loosened his new shoes, admitting air against his sweated socks and feet. His feet freed from shoes altogether, he flexed his toes in open air.

The film was activity again: small faces made large and large places made small in the distortions of a lens. Edmund watched and listened without other patrons speaking from their seats. Nobody walked into or from the seats in rows in front of him, obstructing his view. He could laugh or sigh without other people complaining he disturbed them. He could shout accolades that something was wonderful or profanities that it was not, and nobody would usher him to silence. He could scream love or hate and nobody would know, but he had no need to speak when he could listen to other people.

In the film, an aged widow had spent her life tending to her acorn farm, into which flew a little hummingbird. She talked to it, wanting it to understand her.

Chewing his toffee chocolate and using his tongue to pull it from his teeth when it stuck there, Edmund tried to feel and think the implications of what he watched. He couldn't whisper close to Candice's ear, so not to disturb the other patrons, asking her to explain the film to him. He didn't think that acorn farms were real, which Candice might say was immaterial. He didn't understand the film's title.

Edmund looked up to the beams of coloured lights from the projector, reflected in airborne particles of human dust along their way to the screen. The windows behind him were too high for him to see through them.

He never left a movie part way through it, not wanting to miss anything, but thoughts of anywhere else to go and anything else to do crept into Edmund's mind. Sitting in the dark, his sense of being extraordinary waned. Other people sat alone in city cinemas, watching unpopular movies at unpopular times. His hand explored the darkened seat beside him until it found the plastic bag with the last of his chocolates and more than a dozen empty wrappers. Edmund was doing anything what lonely people did.

They were minor indiscretions, but if he were to frolic in a staid place then he should do so properly. Slowly he stood up, his head casting a shadow at the foot of the big screen. The aged actress continued her performance, until the credits and acknowledgements began scrolling over him.

The last logo finished and the cinema became silent and dark again. The only lights shining were the exit signs above the doors, too weak to illuminate the space around him. Edmund wouldn't return another day to see another lonely movie.

He stepped between the rows of empty seats to the aisle of empty stairs, down which he wandered in the dark. The foyer lights allowed him to see everything again, before he extinguished them, stepped back onto the footpath, and closed the doors behind him. The only remaining place for him to go was his apartment home.

9

SOLITUDE

The windows from the building in which Edmund lived were dark. His car paused before the entrance to the car park, where he passed his home security card over the sensor activating the electric lights in the basement and raising the heavy doors, although the building mightn't have still required their protection. The solitary black car was parked where it had been that morning. Still touching the ceiling was the blue balloon, although it had shrunk since morning. The building rules forbid him doing so, but Edmund parked his car beside the lift instead of his allocated place. The garage doors closed downward and sealed the night outside again.

Edmund donned his jacket into which he slipped his mobile telephone. He took his satchel that had lain inside his car since he left his office and hung it over his shoulder. The lift door opened immediately when he pressed his finger against the button, and he began swinging his shopping bags from his car onto the lift floor, carefully not spilling anything. The lift doors periodically closed before Edmund opened them again, without another person in the building to summon the lift away. The lights automatically switched off, but Edmund pressed the large white button by the lift to activate them again. He locked his car from habit more than caution, before stepping between the bags cluttering the lift floor.

A button on the second floor wall switched on the corridor lights. Through several struggling journeys, Edmund's twisting fingers hauled his unwieldy bags to the floor outside his apartment, before the light reached its allotted time and expired.

Edmund unlocked the door of his dark apartment and pressed the lounge room light switch. The answering machine display by his home telephone still read "0." He didn't switch off that telephone as he usually did at night. His mobile telephone he placed in its small charging unit connected to an electrical socket, recharging the battery overnight.

His satchel lay again in the hallway of his home, while he brought the bags into his kitchen and closed and locked the apartment door. The groceries and household items he'd brought home crammed their appointed shelves and drawers of Edmund's refrigerator, pantry, and cupboards.

His sunglasses returned to the table near his bed and his jacket to his wardrobe, Edmund wondered when he'd need his wallet or watch again. His money sat in bank accounts he had no reason to retrieve.

The television set again played only static. Edmund inserted a videodisc into the player tray to confirm the set was properly functioning, before switching both off.

Edmund sat again at his computer. Nobody had sent him any mail or acknowledgement of receipt of his that morning. Local news sites remained unchanged, as if no human hand or voice had done anything that day.

Other news services remained unavailable. His electronic gateways closed, Edmund couldn't know what other places were still functioning. He couldn't know where people might still be.

Edmund read minor news he hadn't bothered to examine earlier that day, including criticism that the government's longstanding security alert against terrorist attack created unnecessary concern, without identifying specific threats. He read several obscure items, before bracing himself back in his chair; evenings at home alone often bored him.

His eyes drifted around the room, but he'd read the inscriptions on the framed certificates, ribbons, and trophies too many times to read any of them again. He'd heard enough that day not to play the radio persisting, and had already seen and heard the movies and other music recorded on discs for playing through his entertainment system, filed in logical order on his lounge room shelves. The pointless motions and artificial sounds of computer games were tiresome.

Internet reference sites and search engines answered questions that people asked: what they needed or wanted to know. Some sites were inoperative or inaccessible and might've been for a long time, until one site that Edmund accessed was functioning. "*Where is everyone?*" he typed in the keyboard and the screen.

The site responded with a list of businesses catering to everyone, from calligraphy to playing the guitar.

"*What happened last night?*" he typed.

The site responded with public messages of dates long before that date, most of them New Year's Day. His key words were a joke without an ending. The world of information couldn't give him any answers. Exhausting every variation on a phrase and reference available, he couldn't learn the truth.

Social media were meeting places for people not wanting to meet, professing their feelings and opinions to strangers they couldn't see, abusing others for theirs. Their monikers might be their usual names or ones they chose each time they entered, and never used in other places.

Theory made social media easily accessible to anyone in any place, just as the news services should have been, and Edmund tried to access those catering to people through all the time zones of the earth. "*The page cannot be found. The page you are looking for might have been removed, had its name changed, or is temporarily unavailable.*"

Edmund accessed a local chat room. The unreal rooms gave people grace from reputation, where they knew nothing of each other except the truth and lies they read: people they thought or wished they were, or simply creatures of their fantasies. They hid away alone each time their fingers left their keyboards, and kept their virtual identities secret from people who knew their everyday personas.

He registered himself as Veritas, with the password he always used. An array of pseudonyms and introductory messages appeared before him on the screen, none of them identifying where the author lived. The messages were from people far from the circumstances of his experiences that day, introducing themselves with stories of their lives much like other lives. They were in homes and offices near to or far from his, in quiet moments between chores. The most recent of the messages was twenty-five hours old.

"*Is anyone out there?*" asked Edmund, typing letters when no one else could hear him. He waited, studying the screen for words or symbols in response, a rhythmic pattern of someone's fingers on an isolated keyboard. People might've seen his message as a joke they couldn't care to answer.

A person could direct responses only to the author of a message, forming anonymous acquaintanceships with words between their hidden safety screens or relationships when they recognised the pseudonyms with which they'd previously conversed. The answer to Edmund's question could be a public one on the screen for everyone to read or a private one to his computer box alone.

Edmund replied to the most recent message without interest in that text. "*Are you still there?*" he typed.

Similarly, he responded to the second most recent message in the room. "*Are you still there?*" he typed, searching for reply. "*It's important that I know.*"

No one reading his messages let Veritas know that he or she was there. The people not yet willing to return were somewhere, but Edmund couldn't find them. He shut down his computer.

The quiet brought him back to every other night. Thinking of things to do, the evening was too late to call someone. It was too early for him to sleep.

The thoughts once his were no longer opportune. Edmund once had reason to think of work, but could no longer rush to meeting people. He once could think of things to buy, but had no more call to choose.

He wandered into the lounge room, for the want of anything to do. Hanging from the sheen white walls, contemporary oil paintings of starkly black and coloured lines on canvases might've been interesting to examine, for just a moment. High in the four corners of the walls protruded the small black blocks that were remote small sound speakers for the entertainment system, which filled the cabinet dominating the centre of a wall. The bottles of wine standing on a table were those he and his mother exchanged as presents each Christmas season; buying them was easier than thinking much about them. Edmund scrutinised what he'd never before noticed.

The electric light glistened in the glass atop the grey iron table. It fractured in the small pyramids patterned into a lead-crystal carriage clock. All else had stopped, but the clocks continued turning; the changing time neared ten o'clock. He'd brought the clock with him each time he moved from one apartment into one better than the last during the years of his career, and stood it where it was most visible. It was the most consistent feature of each lounge room, while the furniture became more opulent through changing styles and window views became those of better neighbourhoods.

Edmund studied a glass of tap water in his hand. He smelt it, and smelt it again, assuring himself that it was odourless, before gently tasting it with the tip of his tongue. The water safe to drink yesterday was still safe to drink, but he opened a cold red can of cola from the refrigerator.

One woman leaving him was more profound than had been everybody leaving, but if all other people had remained through a normally working Tuesday while Candice affirmed his fears and declined to see him, then Edmund would still have returned alone to his apartment, drunk that cold cola from a can, and eaten a packaged meal at the dining table in a corner of his lounge room. The freezer contained the frozen food in sealed containers that were his meals alone on ordinary days, cooked according to the simple instructions on the packaging. His time alone was more prolonged than just the hours since Tuesday morning.

The suspension of their lives deferred the conversation she

might've forced them to endure, saving him from hearing what she might or mightn't say. He would want her to remain. She might refuse him. He might consider breaking her photograph and decide he wouldn't, before he slumped alone to bed and woke alone to any day. The day passed had been a holding pattern, a hiatus from the feelings and distractions, but a hiatus nevertheless. Her life had stepped aside without remark.

Finishing his cola, Edmund placed the empty can on the kitchen bench. He would drop it in the bin for recyclable aluminium, when the world of every life returned. The strange story of that day, that day that never was, would end, although not because of anything he did. His time alone might end that minute or might last another day or week.

Edmund stood at his lounge room window, to which the lights of night reflected from other building windows. Throughout the city, night-lights shone in buildings that otherwise were dark. They shone from empty buildings upon empty streets of stones, blazing their imitated grandeur as they blazed it every night. The lights that replicated crowds of people in the offices, once linking disparate cubicles of strangers at their desks, only accentuated the solitude of shadows. Street lights were solitary lights, separated from each other by the darkness of the night.

When he was ten years old, Edmund stared long at that same maze of lights in another electric city. Each afternoon, his parents' only child walked from the stop where the school bus left him to his home, where he inserted each of three keys to unlock the white-painted front door. Responding to the opening door was Martha, a large lumbering woman with burly arms and her black hair tied in a bun. "How was school today, young man?" she always asked, in her thickly accented voice.

"Like yesterday." Edmund left his school bag in his bedroom, took some biscuits from a plate and glass of fruit juice from the kitchen, and watched the television set in the room dedicated to him at the back of the house. Martha's final chore was to prepare the meals that would be the boy's and sometimes his parents' dinners, if they arrived home before Martha left the house.

An unfamiliar tone for a mobile telephone sounded one

afternoon, enticing Martha to hurry into the kitchen and open her large, tawdry black handbag. "Hello," she said.

Young Edmund watched her listening to words he couldn't hear, responding with words he couldn't understand. When she finished, Martha searched her handbag until she pulled from it a small diary. Using the telephone lying on the kitchen bench, she dialled a number from it. "Gwyneth Toomey's office," answered a woman. Edmund could hear the voice coming through the earpiece.

"Mrs Neale?" said Martha.

"Mrs Neale is in a meeting at the moment."

"I must speak to her," persisted Martha. "This is an emergency."

"I'm sorry, but she has left specific instructions not to be disturbed. I can give her a message when she has finished."

"I'll call her husband."

Edmund continued watching her, while she telephoned another number. "Mister Neale's office," another voice replied.

"I must speak to Mister Neale. This is an emergency."

"May I ask who's calling?"

"I'm Mister Neale's housemaid. I'm at his home with his son."

"Please wait while I try to locate him." The line was silent for several minutes. "Putting you through...."

"Yes, Martha," boomed the voice of Edmund's father.

"Mister Neale. One of my children is very sick and I must get home right away. Where can I leave Edmund?"

"Can't someone else look after your child?"

"No, Mister Neale."

"Don't you have other family or neighbours?"

"I must get home, as soon as I can."

"Have you spoken with Mrs Neale?"

"No one will let me speak with her."

"Martha, if you can wait..."

"I must go now, Mister Neale, I must go. I can't leave your son here alone."

Mister Neale sighed. "Get a taxi to bring him here. Have the driver call this number when he's here. My secretary can meet him, pay the fare, and bring him up."

"Thank you, Mister Neale."

Martha arranged what Edmund's father had asked her to arrange. His father's secretary came to the waiting taxi. "You must be Edmund," she smiled.

"Yes, ma'am."

"You call me Julie."

The child from a distant school and home stood at the long glass window in the reception area of his father's offices. In the building across the street, he saw office interiors with people walking and sitting at their desks and tables, an environment for adults, for the first time. They didn't notice him.

The cars and pedestrians below him were much smaller than he was. Young Edmund leant forward to see them better, trying to see the side of the building in which he stood, when his hands touched the glass. "Please don't do that," snapped the woman at the reception desk behind him.

Edmund turned around as she rose from her chair, quickly checked the lifts and corridors, and hurried away. She soon returned carrying a small cloth and a flask, from which she sprayed fluid on Edmund's finger marks he hadn't seen. She wiped the glass clean, removing all trace of his hands. "If you touch anything again," she told him, "I'll need to tell your father."

Young Edmund sat patiently in a brown leather chair, drinking cups of orange juice and eating biscuits that Julie occasionally brought to him. Edmund turned the pages of the magazines resting on the table with him, looking at the pictures. Some men and women surprised to see a child sitting in the reception area smiled at him. "Are you being looked after?" some asked.

"Yes, sir. Yes, ma'am."

"This is Mister Neale's son," explained the woman at the reception desk, without diminishing his solitude.

At six o'clock, she checked that Edmund was still sitting in his chair and left the offices. Waiting until he was certain she was not returning, Edmund returned to the window, careful not to touch the glass. The night was becoming dark, but most offices were still alight. Some people still walked and sat among the desks, although they were much fewer in number than they'd been. A woman took her handbag from a cupboard in her desk and departed.

Behind him, Julie interrupted, dressed in her coat and carrying her bag. "Have you eaten enough, Edmund?" she asked him.

"Thank you, ma'am."

"Your father will be here when he can." She left.

More floors of offices in other buildings became dark, while the boy stood at the window. The longer he stood there, the larger the buildings became. They became stronger in the night, more powerful. Flickering fluorescent lights mesmerised him, until Edmund forgot that he was standing there alone.

Shortly before eight o'clock, dressed in his long coat and carrying his large leather briefcase, Edmund's father appeared from a corridor. "We can go now," he told Edmund.

His father strode to the lift well, while his son hurried to catch him. "I trust Julie looked after you," he said. "Martha should never have put us in this position. This is not why we pay her."

Edmund and his father stood quietly in the lift while it descended. The doors opened on the ground floor of the building and his father stepped out. Edmund followed him around several corners to a smaller lift, which took them down into a car park. "Why do you and mother work?" Edmund asked him, as they sat in his father's car taking them home.

"You like your house, don't you? You like food, everything else we have, don't you?"

"We have them now?"

His father glanced at the dashboard clock, activated the indicator light, and turned the car from the road. "I'll show you," he said, pressing the button locking the car doors.

He drove them into the darker city streets, where buildings were poorly lit and few pedestrians walked. He slowed the car, pausing without stopping his car engine outside a small laneway. A rare light illuminated a large steel garbage bin and several piles of rubbish. Two men wearing long clothes and ragged hats obscuring their faces rubbed their hands and warmed their faces in the steam rising from a round grated vent in the ground. "Do you know what they are Edmund?" asked his father. "They are vagabonds, who wear the rags we throw away or they would die in the cold. They eat the food we give them in restaurant doggie bags: the meals we're too full to finish eating. They live in whatever disused railway tunnel or derelict building they can find. Is that how you want to live? Is that how you want us to live?"

"No, sir."

"You remember the bums you saw tonight and be grateful your parents work as we do," said his father, leaving the illuminated laneway. The only greater inspiration than the lifestyle that wealth could bring was the fear of living in crude poverty, without anything to own.

"I'm sorry, sir."

His father's voice became conciliatory. "Diligent men and women live well, Edmund. Idle men and women don't."

Twelve years later, soon after Edmund started working, his father died, slumped over his office desk. Few of his father's colleagues and commercial confidants attended his funeral, for which his widow asked their only child to speak the eulogy. Edmund wanted to say good things about him, but he didn't know enough to talk about him at his passing. His only knowledge could've been a short newspaper notice of simple public data: the date that he was born; the title of his work; the names of next of kin. He could recall reams of tertiary education, but knew no private sensibilities or anything profound about his father. Two parents he'd rarely seen were not a family he could readily call his own.

Another twelve years later, that empty Tuesday night, Edmund was again looking at lights and darkness. If his father had bequeathed to the universe a soul then Edmund wondered what impression he was making on that soul, in the lifestyle he'd acquired. He reached forward to see the street better, leaning his hands against the window, but the cars and pedestrians had gone.

No longer could Edmund lose his thoughts in conversations and activities, leaving him with nothing much to do but think too much. He disliked memory.

Edmund would save his time awake for the new day coming, whatever that day would be. He removed his trousers and hung them over the chair near his bed, where the air would freshen them overnight, leaving the rest of his worn clothes on the floor. Edmund dressed into his grey tracksuit, switched off the lights of his apartment and then his bedroom, and retired to his bed. He checked the time on the digital clock and would check it again each time he woke during the night and in the morning, dreaming within a dream about people who weren't there.

The carousel had stopped turning for a day and the treadmill had stopped running, but they would be turning and running again soon. The things he hadn't done that day had made him weary.

10

WEDNESDAY MORNING

The radio woke Edmund to the time of every weekday morning, playing another song he'd already heard. What had been too early one day previously was not too early Wednesday morning.

Edmund was slow to leave his bed, because doing so would teach him too much about the day just passed. If he'd dreamt that empty city day, then the day to which he woke was Tuesday real, much like Tuesdays had always been. If lost Tuesday hadn't been a dream, then Wednesday might yet proceed as other days had done.

An ordinary day coming would reveal to him the secrets of Tuesday past. News services published overnight would mention the reason almost everyone had fled, among the reams of expert commentary and residents' reactions. "What did you get up to you yesterday?" Edmund would ask casually in a conversation at the office, taking water from the cooler in the kitchen. "Did you hear the warning, the false alarm?" If he met a man named Cusack then he would ask him what he knew.

The radio finished playing a song and began to play another. Edmund stretched his arm out from his bed and turned the dial, but only static sounded where every other station played. The station to which he'd woken played only music, as it played it yesterday.

The day shone on the streets below his lounge room window, but they were no less empty than they'd been empty yesterday. The few more leaves fallen on the ground had aged by one more day. The rows of trees were motionless, without a breeze to stir them. Small white clouds drifted through the sky. No aircraft surveyed the damage that never happened.

No new electronic mail had come to his computer. Only the dates of days updated automatically had changed in the sites he could access; the weather forecasts had been longer range on Monday evening than they'd become on Wednesday morning. Wednesday would be warmer than Tuesday had been, with the threat of falling rain. The evening would be cool. Edmund seemed to be there every morning, repeating the same thing, thinking the same thoughts.

A song finished and a voice spoke on the radio. Edmund turned around to face the sound coming to him from his bedroom: a recorded advertisement for retirement planning. The day for working was again extraordinary, and he wondered how many days would need to be like those two before the extraordinary became ordinary. The new day was another day with nobody: only the second he'd woken without society, but those days were the only days he knew. He switched off the radio.

Work had been a ritual Edmund accepted when there was nothing else to do, but if he proceeded to his office then he would be working without needing to perform, doing what he'd already done. Showered but unshaven, with the shadows of short hairs and ambiguities they created, Edmund dressed into a spacious shirt and trousers along with walking shoes for days without anyone to meet. He ambled from his apartment, securing the door behind him and wondering why he did.

Only the black car and Edmund's car were in the basement car park, for the second inexplicable day. The blue balloon lay dying on the floor.

Roads had become freeways without imposition from other cars or the rules of many people, in the city that was his. Roadways where middling drivers once queued motionless, Edmund sped as if they were features in a massive stupid fun park. Wholly in control of everything he did, he wantonly cut through corners oblivious to road markings, changing lanes that only he could see. Edmund flouted every law he once heeded, swerving past parked vehicles risking lives that were not there. He could do everything he wanted, revelling in the freedom of a life without constriction.

If Edmund was insane, living a crazy fantasy, then he enjoyed insanity. If he was dreaming, then he didn't want to wake. If he woke from his sleep or recovered from his insanity, then nobody but he would know what he had done inside the trapdoor of his mind. The day was his to do the things he'd never before done. The only acts he might regret would be acts he didn't do.

Defying the place for people no longer there, Edmund surged onto an empty footpath and along it and bounced back over the small kerb, his euphoria of control and recklessness. Signs warning cars away only challenged him to violate them. His car powered over pebbled concrete paving stones to a plaza for pedestrians: an arena for him spinning in his car. He weaved between the trees and sculptures, in a maze that he was making from a pattern in the puzzle, before tiring of the game and bundling his car back to public streets.

Cameras watching him from somewhere didn't care what he was doing and neither did he. He would be best when he'd forgotten the rules that he was breaching.

Ahead of him appeared a familiar several-storey building: a department store. All luxurious necessities that anyone could want waited for him in the store. He'd wanted the best of everything too long a time to stop wanting it too soon.

Edmund stopped his car at the kerb in front of one of the store's wide entrances, sealed by steel shutters. To the sides of them were display windows, in which stood intermittently remodelled wax mannequins of stylised human beings. Edmund stared admiringly at their attire. Wax figures without pride or taste were wasting menswear that Edmund could be wearing with purpose and feeling. They looked past him as if he wasn't there. Perhaps he wasn't.

The store ought to have been open, according to the opening hours marked neatly on the window. Sensors would respond to the windows breaking, activating alarms in the store and a police station or security firm somewhere, with a flashing light and directions for response. Burglars in normal times would flee the noise before police or security guards arraigned them, but the law enforcers weren't there to apprehend.

If Edmund took goods from the shops then he would be like the looters of other people's property in the aftermath of tragedies on the television news. His would be the face and figure that people came to watch, recorded by security cameras Edmund couldn't recall seeing. The police returning to their stations could view the tape and evidence for courts to convict him of a crime, before copying it for the benefit of journalists and media. People like him would watch horrified at what they saw the stranger did, judging and condemning him over coffee drunk for breakfast.

Nobody might return for days or weeks. Rats and bugs might eat the clothes. Moisture might ruin them with mould.

Edmund looked around. The plant pots were too heavy to lift. The litterbin stands were affixed to the ground, but Edmund drew from one the steel bin and emptied its few contents on the ground. He should revel in his experience and, when everyone returned, not rue having had the capacity to do anything but not doing it. His jinks would be the stories he told his new-found friends, in later days when they sat together in reopened city bars; jokers would tease him for not having done more. His young-man stunts would be the material of memories among the old men getting older. He could never do again what he could do that day.

Through the sounds of open air and wind between the buildings, a slighter, indiscernible sound intruded upon his concentration. He'd become accustomed to the silence and might've imagined the noise from his reminiscences, shaking the air around him. The small growing sense of a sound was mechanical, like that of a wayward engine, but coarse. It might've been gradually becoming louder, coming around corners he could see from streets that he could not. The vehicle might've been alone or headed a flotilla invading his realm.

Edmund hurriedly returned the litterbin to the stand and

stepped into the entrance alcove around the shutters, pressing his back and head into the corner. The sound of a vehicle bustling along a street became louder, as he turned his head away, reducing his profile from the road. His heart racing trapped against the wall, the sound continued growing, as the vehicle he couldn't see approached. If it were searching for him, he could say he'd been afraid and not be lying.

The sound peaked and then slowly reduced. Edmund started to relax, but wouldn't turn around. Standing rigid in the shadow, he waited, until the noise became a memory. Slowly he ventured his face out, and saw he was alone.

The stores were waiting for him to conquer; everything expensive his to take. Edmund recovered the litterbin, stepped towards the glass, and held it above his head with both his hands, more like a circus strongman than a company executive. Edmund had never thrown anything like that but had seen images in movies of musclemen throwing things; he could do anything that actors could.

Within the display window weren't just well-clothed mannequins but black fabric-covered shelves decorated with Royal Delft porcelain. There was no reason for him to break it but the power in him to do so. Edmund smiled, knowing what he was about to do. In the motion with which he was intrinsically conversant, he threw the bin against the window.

A thousand loud alarms blasted sirens through the air, a whirlwind made in hell. Reeling backwards, Edmund's hands pressed hard against his poor shocked ears to try to block the racket, while shattered glass sprayed into the store and the steel bin fell to earth. The raging sirens reverberated through his head and body, the shops and city, while Edmund scarpered away.

They screamed for several minutes before suddenly abating, when the noise pollution laws no one remained to implement required the sound to cease. The street was again quiet, beautifully quiet, but for Edmund collecting the last of his breath and the nerves inside his head. He pulled his hands from his ears and saw what he had done. In the centre of a spiralling web to the corners of the remnant windowpane, spikes of crackled glass defined a small hole, opening everything beyond it. "Whoa!" he would've yelled and clenched his fists proudly in the air, but he didn't want a security camera recording it.

He'd wrecked the cleanliness. Making an impression was all Edmund ever hoped his work would do.

The senseless faces of the mannequins remained unaffected. The sirens could not be louder than they'd already been, and Edmund picked up the bin and struck the jagged glass repeatedly, making space and scattering more fragments to the floor. The sirens screamed again, but knowing the noise would soon desist made the pounding easier to bear. He remained amidst the mayhem, grimacing as if doing so might block the noise from his hurting head, until he'd enlarged the hole enough for him to drop the bin.

Careful not to cut his clothes or skin and trying not to let the noise deafen him too much, he climbed up and through the space where the window had been, past the knives of fractured glass and idiot mannequins. His arm knocked a shelf of ornaments and a row of tiny porcelain shoes slipped onto the floor, but the sirens were too loud for him to hear them landing.

Edmund clamoured through a black curtain in the corner of the display area into the dark and broken store. The sounds of sirens were trapped with him, and his hands covered his ears for small relief.

The period the noise persisted seemed less the second time. Edmund rested his hands from his ears, relaxing his arms down to his sides. The silence afresh was tranquillity again.

Draping the curtain to one side admitted a little daylight to the store. With that light and a few night lights inside the store, he found a panel of switches near the entranceway.

Fluorescent lights again blazed overhead, reflected from glass displays and shining floors. Edmund slowly turned around. The high ceiling and wide walls defined a minor universe: the first of several floors of racks and stacks of shelves. Glistening treasures and trinkets surrounded him: the fashions and the wares. For his time alone among them, they were his. Edmund had never before been so rich.

The escalators between floors were idle. Edmund knelt down

to the floor and pressed the button starting the stairs rolling. Starting each flight of escalators and riding them to the rising storeys of the store, Edmund gazed from high upon the floors he'd already seen, with all the power and privilege of a person owning everything he saw.

Edmund browsed as shoppers did, but with the freedom of all choice that only the richest men and women understood. The wools were lush against his hands, soft cashmere with smooth oils. People earning too much money should appear successful.

Amidst the most immaculately tailored suits for every season and stylish shirts that any man could don, Edmund chose clothes that he admired before checking the labels for their prices to know they were the most expensive; a cotton shirt too affordable he replaced on a rack. He wouldn't waste his time and chance with anything he ordinarily bought.

Edmund removed his shoes and draped his shirt and trousers over a customer's chair, unabashed to stand inside a store wearing only his singlet and underpants, before dressing into a new blue shirt and lavish velvet navy-blue suit. The jacket was a little tight on him, so he took one for his sized self. Store assistants had previously helped him choose his ties, but Edmund ventured to golden colours in an interlocked design accentuating his style of suit, he thought.

A dark blue woollen coat augured well for cooler days, hanging long towards his shoes. A fine English umbrella with a tanned leather handle would keep rain from his head and from his new burgundy leather briefcase. Edmund stood before a tall mirror modelling his new appearance: lines and cuts of fabric perfect in reflection, a fashion made for him. He stepped back and to the side, stretching one leg and then the other, bending his arm in dapper poses in the silver portrait glass.

The silks once spun by worms tickled his fingertips. A camel-hair cardigan was almost oily. He placed a pair of deerskin driving gloves firmly on his hands, flexed his fingers in them, and felt each flesh moulded to the other. The clothes Edmund took filled the largest store bag.

Among the watches on mounts in glass cabinets, the finest Swiss watches rested on green cloth in a glass-topped counter.

Looking through the counter glass, he chose a gold Vacheron Constantin, with diamonds and rubies in a gold case on a brown crocodile-skin strap. The most exquisite watches lay before him, but he couldn't touch them. He'd bought less but held more in his hands at the Tiffany's jewellery store, New York than he could take with him that day.

Edmund stood behind the counter where only store assistants normally stood and tried to open the small doors. They remained steadfastly closed. Store attendants had locked the cabinets and counter to safeguard them from thieves, but Edmund was not a thief. He was the owner of the store, who'd let employees enjoy a day away from work. He thought of summoning an assistant back to work, but would leave her to her holiday. He was loath to damage his property any more than he had done.

The locks behind the counter might've been strong enough only to fetter fast hands in the crowd and not been so strong as to prevent a man with time to break them. Edmund placed his right hand on a small handle on a small door behind the counter and tugged it towards him, trying to force it from its lock. The counter started to come towards him and he steadied it with his left hand. His back arched as he forced the handle, until the small door snapped open.

His hand reached through the back of the counter, held the watch he wanted, and carefully lifted it away. He strapped his new watch around his wrist and revered both of them. His old watch he slipped into a pocket of his shirt.

The exquisite ornaments included a sterling silver item Edmund only identified by the unflattering brandy glass whose base rested in its semi-circular silver rim. Below the widest part of the suspended glass was a white cloth wick protruding from a small silver receptacle, joined to the rim with two curling rounded silver rods that formed the sturdy frame. Inflammable fluid in the receptacle would soak through the wick and support a flame, warming brandy in the glass. (Brandy exuded a deeper, more rounded bouquet when warm.)

The warmer was surprisingly heavy when Edmund took it in

his hand. The most reckless of extravagances, he couldn't help but caress it. Without the glass, it fitted in his briefcase.

Elegant pipes hung from hooks on a timber-panelled wall of the tobacconist. A glass-covered counter displayed dozens of thick and thin, short and long cigars, for friends resting in their clubs. Edmund only smoked cigars in his most relaxed of evenings, of which there'd been too few, but he reached down to the shelves below the counter and removed the most elaborately bound box. He broke the seal and raised the lid.

Without cellophane to smother it, the soothing aroma of dried tobacco rose from fifty leaf-wrapped handmade cigars. Close to his nose, their tobacco-field perfume was mystical: an intoxicating cloud inside his head. Using a pair of cigar scissors, he cut the closed end of one cigar. He lit a match and slowly rotated the other end of the cigar in the flame until it charred. He placed the cut end of the cigar on his precious lips, holding the flame a short way from the charred end. Savouring every sense rising through his brain, he drew the warm taste of spice and Cuba to his mind.

Edmund enjoyed the arrogance of being there, of smoking cigars in a place not for smoking them; public law and the department store prohibited him from smoking in that confinement. Store assistants would have run towards him rebuking him and he laughed at them for their concern. The smoke could activate a fire alarm in the ceiling high above him, whereby the storm of water from the ceiling sprinklers would be a rainfall spectacle to behold, during the ruckus of trumpeting fire alarms throughout the store and in an empty fire station. The store was his purveyance to use as he decided and Edmund didn't need to care. More than his domain, it was his plaything. He could find most items in a dozen other stores and if the waterfall ruined everything then he would lose only the convenience of them being in one place.

Without a cleaner close to hand, the store his to soil as he saw fit was also his to keep. Rather than let black ash and a cigar be dirty litter on the floor of his possession, Edmund took a shining ashtray. His longest finger tapped his hot cigar, until another cylinder of black-grey ashen waste crumbled into it.

Leisurely carrying his ashtray but leaving his shopping bag, briefcase and umbrella behind, Edmund read the directory on a board beside the escalators and proceeded to the floor for furniture. Rested in a leather armchair, he calmly watched the soft dots of tiny flames and rising dreamy smoke. His lungs breathed more smoke and his mouth blew it forward into air. His pursed lips couldn't make rings from the smoke, but he had time to practice.

The incongruity amused him. Sitting in that chair among a plethora of chairs wasn't mere defiance of other people's rules, for chairs were made for sitting and cigars were made for smoking. Edmund was being brazen by the normalcy in which he sat to smoke, as if retired to his drawing room. He could well fall silently asleep if he reclined there long enough.

The last ash of his cigar butt left burning in the ashtray by the chair, Edmund pressed the button for a lift, irritated to wait for it to come. Pale wooden panels gentrified the steel box that carried him back to retrieve his new possessions.

The rest of his treasury of spoils remained on shelves and in cabinets. His old clothes remained on a chair. He was the richest man alive: able to take everything he once dreamed of buying and to leave what he might take another time.

The sirens of the store resounded a final time as Edmund, dressed in his new clothes and watch and carrying his shopping bag, briefcase, and umbrella, stepped from the ledge back to the footpath, the smooth soles of his new shoes nearly slipping. The store lights would shine and escalators roll away all day and night for him to see and ride again when next he came, to take some more of everything. He could wear the best each day, discarding the best of yesterday for a new best of tomorrow.

He'd become the king of market town, without consequence or need for sanction. Nobody could stop him doing anything or judge him for having done it. He could do more than he'd ever before thought to do, alive beyond the aspirations that he once had for being alive. In front of him his car, a once expensive green sedan, was not the car he wanted.

11

THE INTRUDER

The streets beckoned cars at Edmund's control, but his was not the most stylish in the city. Rich men bought luxury cars to maintain or appreciate their values over time, driving them fast enough for their ambitions on motorways but not normally on lesser roads.

His department store acquisitions on the passenger seat beside him, Edmund drove his sedan to a Porsche showroom to which his eyes once drifted while waiting in traffic. He parked facing the glass-fronted treasury of sleek, shining vehicles. Edmund removed his sunglasses to see them as they were: the most technically brilliant cars designed and built, better than anything he'd hoped to buy.

Large colourful posters of motor-racing champions in clean white overalls and their sponsors' logos adorned the wall behind the cars. Tall, tropical green trees stood in pots between the posters and in the back corners of the showroom, exuding exotic wilds and pleasure.

The large sliding glass doors allowed the cars to enter and leave the showroom. Smaller hinged doors were for people to come and go. All the doors were surely locked fast, without a garbage bin or other battering tool at hand.

From his seat secure in his old car, Edmund's absent hands

restarted the engine and engaged the gears. He gently pressed his foot down on the accelerator pedal, driving his car slowly across the footpath until its front bumper touched the glass frontier. Only one large sliding door, from ceiling to the floor, kept him and the cars apart.

Inside the long clear taunting wall of doors and windows, a sensor to the left wall and small metal box to the right evidenced an invisible beam a foot above the floor. If the sensor beam was broken, the alarm would sound, although perhaps after a period as much as a minute. That allowed an employee who broke the beam by unlocking and opening the door to reach the large metal box affixed to the wall at the rear of the room and deactivate the alarms. The lock on the box required a key. Beside it, a pad of digits and symbols required a combination of numbers.

Edmund's foot softly pressed the pedal of his car, but the bolts and locks inside the showroom doors stopped his car from moving. Pressing the pedal a little harder, his car front he couldn't see edged forward, straining the tall, wide glass into a yielding arc. The showroom glass squeaked as it bent, until suddenly it shattered with a shriek of twisted sliver and the locks broke away. Alarms exploded acclaiming him, that heraldic commotion hailing him, as Edmund pulled his foot from the accelerator pedal to the brake. The once clean plate of glass was a thick, shining fractured web of a million crossing cracks, but hadn't broken.

Sirens continued to wail but they were unimportant. Edmund again pressed his foot on the accelerator pedal. The shattered glass arced deeper to the strain, fighting him, as he pushed his old car further forward into the complex web, willing the tortured glass to break without damaging the prize it guarded with its life. Nothing could stop his car and him.

Finally, the arcs of glass broke loose from the edges of the pane and fell apart, spilling tiny pieces on the bonnet of his car and on the showroom floor. If they damaged one car's sheen then he would take another. Edmund reversed his car back across the footpath to the street, away from the screaming loud alarms.

The noise of meek alarms continued, while Edmund stepped outside. His index finger of one hand held his new jacket draped over his right shoulder as he stood casually beside his car, gazing towards the open showroom, waiting patiently.

The alarms stopped sounding. The world was again quiet. Edmund carefully stepped over the broken glass into the showroom, where he inspected every car. He reached the last, inspected it, and again inspected others, before finally settling on a red cabriolet: a model 911. Delicately he removed fragments of broken glass without scratching the bonnet, before softly rubbing his clean hand on the smooth, shining paintwork.

People looking to buy cars drove them to test their performance. They drove Porsche cars for the experience. The showroom cars were thus roadworthy. Edmund brought his coat, jacket, and briefcase from his old car to the new, laying them on the seat for a passenger he might never have. He stood his umbrella and laid his shopping bag on the car floor. The key wasn't in the ignition lock.

Against the wall at the showroom rear, two tall cabinets contained only brochures and technical specifications; Edmund had made his decision. The top of the large timber desk near them was empty and the drawers in which dealers might've kept car keys were locked. Behind the desk were two doors on which Edmund turned the handles, but they were also locked. The only unlocked doors were to washrooms.

Edmund leant against a desk front and thrust it across the floor towards one locked door. All the weight and force of the desk and him crashed through one corner of the desk into the door, which creaked and splintered but remained closed. Edmund recovered his energy and aggression, before dragging the desk back from the door. He again thrust the corner of the desk against it, his hands releasing the desk as the battered door splayed open, without alarms bothering to sound.

He pulled the desk aside and stepped into the newly open office. Hanging from the wall behind another desk was a small cabinet, with a door that opened easily in his hand. Hanging from small hooks in the cabinet were several keys with labels identifying cars. The key for his new car was all the power he needed.

Edmund released the bolts fastening the broken showroom door to the floor and ceiling. He pushed the heavy sliding door away. With the tips of his new shoes, he pushed a little of the broken glass across the floor, clearing a path for his new wheels they didn't need.

The leather upholstery exuded its freshly minted aroma, as Edmund reclined low in the driver's seat. Turning his key, the dashboard came alive. Turning it further, he ignited the engine, which stirred through the chassis of his car and seats warmly massaging him. He switched on the radio and heard only noise, before adjusting the reception frequency wanting music. "Are you looking for that someone special in your life?" asked a perennial recorded voice. Edmund switched off the radio.

The steering wheel and gear stick felt his hands through them, as Edmund led his open-roofed new car smoothly into the light and breeze of day. He drove past his former car too easily, turned effortlessly, and cruised away. Sunglasses shielded his eyes while the wind of power in abandon blew at his hair and face, becoming faster and better for everything he did. He and his unstoppable fast car glided through the air, forcing the world behind them in their wake. The car was his best friend and confidant, whom he loved and which loved him. An awesome extension of himself, his car was he.

On the road far ahead of him, sunlight briefly flashed, as if reflected. Edmund slowed a little, but continued driving towards it. Slowly he discerned a car, a bright yellow car, paused part way across an intersection, blocking his path. Standing by the car was a man. Edmund slowing his car until it stopped in the middle of the street.

The man was no more than twenty years old, as tall as Edmund but lean and gaunt with locks of lengthening hair. His clothes were too commonplace to have been stolen from a store that day.

More insolent than threatening, he swaggered without authority towards Edmund, who stepped out of his car. Leaving the door open, Edmund stepped towards him, defending his car from the young man getting close. "What are you doing here?" asked Edmund.

The young man stopped. "The same as you," he replied. "Nice car."

"What's your name?"

"I like my privacy."

"I could memorise the registration number of your car and find someone who could use it to identify you," threatened Edmund.

"That car might be reason for me not to tell you my name."

"Your car is stolen?"

"Isn't yours?"

"Not anymore."

The young man smiled. "Possession is ownership, isn't it?"

"You could make up a name to tell me."

"I don't like to lie," insisted the young man. His point of principle made him seem to Edmund more arrogant than honourable. "I would rather not say anything than say something untrue."

"What should I call you?"

"Call me whatever you want."

"Do you know where everyone is?" asked Edmund.

"That wasn't the first question you asked when you saw me, was it?"

"Do you know where everyone is?"

The strange young man stared at Edmund, flashing his eyebrows upward as he grinned. "How much do you know?" he asked.

"An old woman told me yesterday there was a warning Monday night."

The young man waited, but Edmund had nothing more to say. "To think of all the people talking, and none of them talking to you," the young man pondered. "I thought everyone told somebody, but nobody told you."

"Told me what?"

The young man laughed. "How important is it for you to know?"

"It's important."

"Is it more important to you than your car?"

Edmund felt the young man baiting him, not telling him anything. "Am I in danger?" he asked.

"Are you the only person here?"

"Are we in danger?"

"What people once thought might kill them mightn't kill us now," said the young man, relieving Edmund from too much fear. "We're not about to die, not this minute anyway, but other people might disagree, mightn't they?"

Edmund's composure firmed, refusing to let the intruder enjoy advantage over him. "Why did everyone leave?"

"You should've seen it: people driving their cars, rushing to railway stations, catching buses in the night, too scared to say anything too loudly."

"Is the emergency over?" asked Edmund.

"Do you mean a real emergency, or one that people thought was real?" The young man started walking slowly around Edmund and his car, keeping his distance from them. "You have everything but knowledge. All the nice things you can touch, your car and clothes, can't tell you facts that you don't know."

Edmund also turned, always facing him and keeping himself between the young man and his car. Edmund's new possessions lay exposed on the passenger's seat and floor.

"You've been shopping," said the young man.

"Is that your business?"

"Testy, testy," the young man dismissed him. "I saw the showroom. Did you forget your key?"

"I've had enough of this..."

"Maybe I should warn you, but not about the things you think you should be warned."

"What else is there?"

"Imagine me, young me, warning old you about anything."

"I'm not old."

"You're older than I am. That makes you old. I wonder if someone will warn me when I'm as old as you are now, or if you've already warned me."

"Your antics are wasting time."

"Time?" retorted the young man. "We always have time, whatever we do with it. I might enjoy teasing you."

"I don't," said Edmund, returning to the driver's door of his car. "Goodbye."

"You and I are the only people here and you're going?"

"You'll find someone else."

"*You* might not."

Edmund's hand was on his open door. He turned back to face the stranger.

"I can find other people, I know where they are. I can find people like you, but people like you can't find people like you. You think you're unique, but you're not. You think you're special, and you might be special, but that doesn't make you unique. Even when you find people like you, you don't know what to say to them. You don't know what to say to me. You might never know."

The young man might've insulted him. Edmund started to sit in his car.

"I can tell you what you know," the young man quickly added, "but you'll have to give me something. You have to pay for what you want."

Edmund evaluated the young man's tone before believing him. The young man had no reason to be generous. "What do you want?" asked Edmund, standing up again.

"What do you have?"

"I have everything."

"I don't want everything. I don't want the trouble of trying to keep it."

"What do you want?"

"I want your car."

"No."

"You don't own it," said the young man. "It's registered in a name that isn't yours. Eventually, you'll be forced to give it back."

"You can't have it."

"You can get another one."

"No." Confident in his position, Edmund negotiated as he negotiated in his career.

The young man stood silently, before stepping closer to Edmund's car. "Show me what you have," he said.

Edmund looked down beside the driver's seat and quickly recognised the clearly marked small levers. He reached down and pulled one, causing the car bonnet to slip from its lock and catch.

The young man wouldn't open it. Instead, he stepped back, giving Edmund space, watching him.

Edmund closed the driver's door, walked around the car, and lifted the bonnet. He stepped back to let the young man see that the luggage compartment was empty.

The young man moved around the car to the passenger's seat. Edmund could easily replace his coat and jacket from the store, as he could the contents of his shopping bag the young man picked up, looked inside, and returned; clothes that fitted Edmund mightn't fit the leaner man. He opened Edmund's briefcase. "What's this?" he asked, picking up a shining silver ornament.

Edmund pushed the car bonnet closed. "A brandy glass warmer."

"I'll have that."

"What would you do with a brandy glass warmer?" Young men didn't drink brandy.

"You stole it."

"Here," said Edmund, raising his arm, pulling his sleeve, and showing the young man the watch on his wrist. "This is more useful and much more expensive." He removed the watch from his wrist and held it up.

The young man studied the watch and Edmund encouraging him to take it. "I want the brandy glass warmer."

"You only want it because I want it."

"That's my offer," insisted the young man. "I'll tell you what you want to know if you give me the warmer."

"This is ludicrous," snapped Edmund. "I'm offering you something worth far more..."

"Then you're ludicrous for making the offer. Prices don't matter when you can have everything you want, only when you can't."

Edmund deliberated upon how much he wanted to learn about events since Monday night. Another stranger might already be approaching, although Edmund couldn't hear it. Somebody eventually would tell him what he wanted to know, but he might never again see such a treasure as that silver warmer. "No deal," he said, buckling his watch back around his wrist. The watch secure, he stretched his arm towards the warmer in the young man's hands. "Give that back to me."

The young man clutched it to his chest. "You took it from someone. I'm taking it from you."

"It's mine," said Edmund. "I earned it."

The two men glared at each other, until Edmund tried to grab the warmer. The young man pulled the warmer harder to his chest as he stepped towards his car, but Edmund grabbed the young man's arm with one hand and grappled for the warmer with the other. The young man's hand locked on the warmer while he struggled to escape, the two men wrestling their arms and hands trying to take and trying to keep the silver trinket. The young man writhed as they fought frantically together, pulling at the warmer and pushing at each other until the young man fell against Edmund's car. Edmund pulled them from the car without risking harm to his warmer, dragging them to the ground, scratching their legs and waist against the street through their quickly fraying clothes. They grappled until together they knelt bundled on the ground when, embarked upon a rage, Edmund shook the young man trying to hurt him, trying to shake loose the young man's grip around the silver. The young man only needed to escape with it, pushing Edmund's face fending him away.

The young man forced himself upright, but Edmund holding fast rose with him until they stood wreathing together in a single torturing mass. They brawled ferociously, with Edmund's piercing eyes focussed on that warmer his hands couldn't quite grasp. Muscles burned and seethed, driving limbs against stretched skin prodding for a small point of lost control. The warmer was too small for two men to hold, but Edmund's hand grabbed part of it and his other hand tried to prize the young man's fingers from it.

One structure in their vicious embrace, with gritted teeth and aching faces, they stared down the shining warmer they both held close to them. Their tautly muscled necks jostled with each other but their labours kept them almost motionless, with every movement to the silver slow, long, and forced. The sides of the young man's hands dug deep at Edmund's cheek, pinching his flesh against the bones of his sore jaw. Their desperate, rough struggle immersed their bitter minds and bodies, where pain was just more reason to punish the other.

They were binding each other's hands to the hard silver and trying to push the other's hands and arms away from it. The young man gripped doggedly, as determined to keep what could be his to own as Edmund was to recover what he knew was his. Only the warmer was important, and if Edmund needed to break the stranger's fingers to possess it then he would do so without compunction. The only taper on his struggle was trying not to break, bend, or dent the warmer, but if their battle damaged it, then in vengeance Edmund left to hold the broken trophy would thump the man who'd ruined it.

The young man's obsession might've wavered as his hands began to fail him, spurring Edmund to new strength in his ambition. Edmund's hands became stronger on the silver, and when his grip was strong enough, his other hand pushed like a punch against the young man's chest, forcing him to stagger backwards and almost fall. The warmer was again Edmund's, but his fury made him the victor reach forward and push again, driving the vanquished stumbling down onto the street. The two men were panting, but gripping the silver in his hand, Edmund stood poised to fight again if the young man again threatened his possession.

"Keep the damned thing," the young man screamed from the street. "It's a brandy glass warmer. It doesn't mean a thing. What would you or I do with a brandy glass warmer?"

Recovering his breath more gradually than was the younger man, Edmund relaxed his grip enough to check the warmer was intact, before securing it in his briefcase. His finger ran over the smooth paintwork of his car where the two of them had tussled. He couldn't feel a dent.

"I'll tell them about you," the young man still lying on the ground called out. "I'll tell them you're mad, you're dangerous, but you're worse than that: you're pitiful, or at least you would be if anybody cared enough to pity you." The young man examined his hands and legs. They weren't bleeding.

Edmund brushed the dust from his hands, shirt, and trousers. His hands combed down the hair ruffled from his head and wiped the perspiration from his brow. He straightened his tie. The watch on his wrist was unscratched.

"They might all be hiding from you," the young man resumed. "I might be the only person game to see you. Have you thought about that?" His eyes glanced up at the windows overlooking them. "Or are you hiding from them?"

Edmund couldn't believe anything he said. Standing at his driver's door, he pressed the button unfolding the car roof from behind the seats. Fully stretched, it reached the windscreen top and enclosed the space for people. He closed the windows.

The young man stood up from the road. Watching Edmund watching him, warding him away, he too patted down his shirt and trousers. He retreated to his yellow car, started it, and turned to drive away. The car became smaller between the city blocks of buildings, until it turned around a corner and Edmund couldn't see it anymore. The bumbling of its engine receded, dissipating, until it too had gone.

Edmund's breath slowly recovered from his joust, until he could no longer hear it. No cars emitted sounds he heard. No more men appeared to challenge him. The soothing sounds of the background city breeze affirmed he was again alone, but the fight had left his new clothes clammy.

12

THE CITY MANSION

The time had come to rest, but Edmund's empty small apartment would not suffice as the victor's rooms and board. A hotel long regarded as one of the finest in the city was better suited to a man of his new stature: the lord of crystal manor.

Most accommodation was in the taller structure of the hotel, built within and above the old stone-arched surrounds. A forecourt of dark cobblestones heralded the wide stone steps leading up to the hotel doors, open every day and late at night. Shining lobby lights invited Edmund in.

Edmund parked his car at the foot of the steps for the valet to take away. He locked the doors to keep his car secure from rogues on his estate.

Wearing his new jacket and coat, Edmund carried his shopping bag, briefcase, and umbrella up to the hotel doors, unconcerned that he had not reserved a room. Without the doorman in his black and gold uniform in attendance, Edmund pushed open a door with his shoulder. Without porters in sight, he rested his small luggage on a tall trolley.

The pale polished foyer floor was pristine clean and sparkling. Old paintings and tapestries adorned the walls, behind round Corinthian columns holding up the roof. A crystal chandelier shone from the centre of the ceiling, from which spread scrolls and leaves of art.

Without well-groomed clerks behind the reception desk, Edmund stood in their stead. He dragged a computer mouse across the colourful mouse mat beside a keyboard, triggering the screen to life.

The computer was operational without need for passwords, as it would've been for late night guests registering into the hotel and early morning people checking out. Computer programmers had made most tasks easy to undertake, with prompts and cursors in simple language set out on the screen. Edmund typed his most logical suppositions of requisite words and codes into the keyboard, until he identified the best room in the hotel: the Presidential Suite. The room was available that night, its tariff exorbitant for anyone but him.

Edmund started typing his name as that of the guest, but the hotel manager unaware of his status might later invoice him for the tariff. He deleted the letters he'd typed, and recorded the guest's name in the space on the screen as being "*to be advised.*" The computer required a date at which he would leave the suite, and Edmund nominated the day one week later. He could extend that date if it arrived without anyone at the hotel offending him by questioning anything he did, or by threatening to take away his room. The computer offered him newspapers, included in the tariff, and Edmund accepted each publication every day, delivered to his suite. He pressed the key to activate the small machine on a shelf below the desk, which churned out the plastic cards admitting guests into their rooms for the periods they were registered.

A steel lift carried Edmund and his trolley to the highest floor of the hotel. Pushing the trolley ahead of him, he stepped onto soft, smooth carpet in a wide corridor. Small lights gently illuminated the plush red paper on the walls, in the felt overlay of which weaved stylised floral patterns. Double dark timber doors with shining brass door handles stood closed before him, but Edmund pressed the plastic card into the slot above one handle and the bolt clicked unlocked. He turned the handle and pushed open the door.

The plush red wallpaper in the sitting room was the same as in the corridor, but with small brass lights illuminating classical oil paintings. The dark-stained oak furniture was immaculate and the lighting from the ceiling soft and supple. The palatial suite was for political and business leaders as well as famous actors and actresses, but none of them was as rich as Edmund had become. He rested his bag and briefcase on the floor and leant his umbrella against them. He loosened the strap of his new watch and sat it upright on a table. He'd found his new abode.

The high vantage of his mansion home revealed a view across the placid city; below lines of empty building tops were lines of empty streets. Buildings were steppingstones for lesser giants, markers for their dancers, and Edmund was their audience to see what none of them was doing, outside his mansion window. The man who'd tried to steal from him might've been inside a home among the rockwork, as might've been other survivors in the city, or might've come to the city centre from the suburbs and returned there.

Dominating the master bedroom was a bed four thick down pillows wide, cloaked in a woollen spread and below a crafted bedhead and canopy. Edmund removed his coat, jacket, and tie and hung them in a cupboard, without reason to live anywhere else again.

In the sitting room, a wooden cabinet concealed shelves of liquid spirits and a small refrigerator. Champagne was for the most decadent of celebrations and the Krug was renowned. Edmund removed the wire seal and foil wrapper over the cork and held his hands over the bottleneck, where his thumbs in little motions from the glass slowly pushed up the cork. The pressure of the bubbles in the bottle began to push with him, when suddenly the cork exploded from the bottle and knocked against the ceiling. The cold froth and bubble ran over Edmund's hands, down to the rug beneath him, as the cork fell beside the window.

To use and idly waste as rich men did, Edmund laughed at the mess he'd made for a stranger someday to clean. He poured the Champagne into a wide, shallow Champagne glass, spilling some of it onto the cabinet. His pursed lips sucked some liquid heaven, from which the bubbles rose through him.

Also in the cabinet were little vacuum-sealed glass jars of tiny black and red fish eggs. Edmund unfastened a lid, letting the freshness of black caviar breathe out. He dipped into it a silver knife, removed a serving of the delicacy, and gently set it on a little square of complimenting toast from a plastic packet. The eggs broke open in his mouth and spilled the rich juices between his teeth and tongue. Opening a second jar, red caviar was perhaps more mellow than the black. The pale crumbs of toast conspicuously spilled on a mahogany round table.

Carrying his glass of cool Champagne in one hand and small jar of coloured fish eggs in the other, Edmund stood at the open door of his mammoth pale-tiled bathroom, around which were spread a glass-walled shower, a large spa bath, and a long ordinary bath. A large, clear mirror stood over the vanity unit and two porcelain washbasins, making everything brighter in reflection than it was directly to observe. The tap handles and pouring spouts were formed from polished brass. Edmund was on the best of holidays, in a lifestyle to which he only had aspired, but to which he already was accustomed.

Usually he showered, cleaning himself quickly, but he had no more call to hurry. Baths were for leisure, relaxation, and pleasure, and no baths more so than the spa bath presented to Edmund in his suite.

Hot water billowed from the bath taps, exuding steam into the air. Bubbles larger and more turbulent than those in the Champagne glass blew into the water. Undressed, the frothing water massaged Edmund's muscles.

Lying in his bubbling bath water with his bubbles of Champagne and a small silver entrée fork, Edmund nibbled at the fish eggs from a jar. People once envied other people living as he was living and he'd been among the envious, but he became indifferent to what was easy for him, as the truly rich were. Beyond decadence, he enjoyed himself and that was all to which most people had aspired, with everything he wanted. The bath became full and spa bubbles stopped when he tired of the activity, leaving only the water trickling from his skin.

Edmund was experiencing something unique he didn't understand; his future brought upon him fast. The day was the most glorious of his life, doing all he could do and leaving nothing he could've done undone. He wanted more days, weeks or months perhaps, living as he was living, before the people he once knew wandered back.

He wouldn't return to his office job and time except in his society. He may not return to it even then.

The skin on his moist fingers started to crease, and Edmund released the brass-covered rubber plug. The sounds of cooling water drained from his bath and more water dripped from his body when he stood upright and stepped onto a mat. A long white bathrobe in which was embroidered the gold crest of the hotel was soft against his skin and he knotted the cord around his waist. Removed from their plastic packaging, the white cloth hotel slippers were no less gentle around his feet. He poured more cold Champagne into his glass.

Wearing his robe and slippers and a cool Champagne glass in hand, Edmund wandered from his suite to explore his mansion palace: the completeness of his achievement. The lift carried him back down, to where the lounge bar was quiet, as such bars rarely were. Edmund stood in that public place wearing only his private robe and slippers because he was free to do so.

A man in a tuxedo had played the grand piano the last time he was there. A woman in a long black dress sometimes stood near him, singing words to melodies of music, while patrons talked between themselves and sometimes listened. Without talking guests and serving waiters, Edmund could rest there undisturbed.

Sitting at the piano, Edmund raised the lid, revealing the long row of thick ivory and thin black keys. He tapped them, but failed to play. Extracting melodies from notes demanded talent he didn't have.

At one end of the long row of keys was a switch, which Edmund flicked, releasing familiar tones and chords in unison with the keys moving down and up again. The pianist wasn't playing, but the instrument persevered.

Edmund walked around the bar, sometimes moving with the

rhythm, doing anything he decided to do. He sung lyrics to melodies he recognised through the renditions as loudly or softly as he wanted his contribution to be, without anyone preventing him from hearing his small voice. The sounds he made and motions he performed were unabashed, free to be everything and anything, unaffected and unconcerned by other people. If the voice he heard was his then it didn't embarrass him.

The piano played another encore: more tunes he recognised from the background to conversations in lounge bars and restaurants somewhere. From a window of the place in which he'd come to live, Edmund looked upon the grounds of his estate: the empty city street outside. He straightened his bathrobe over him.

In a corner of the bar was an entertainment system more precise, articulate, and honest than the one in his apartment. Among the discs of recorded music were the varied works of bands and lyricists, folk singers strumming their guitars and orchestras, for the range of customer tastes. Among the discs was a recording of classical music by Johann Sebastian Bach.

Edmund stopped. The music impressed upon the disc might've included compositions he could've heard with Candice. He read the cover as he would've read the programme on Monday evening.

The piano played music he could hear at any time. Edmund switched it off.

Doing what he could only do in the city without people, he found the system speakers and stood them at the open window, directing them outside. He pressed a button with the symbol for opening trays for discs and an empty tray slid open. The tips of his fingers held the edges of the Bach as if the disc were his, careful not to let his fingers tarnish the information surfaces while he withdrew it from the plastic case. He placed the disc on the tray, pressed the button closing it, and pressed the button rotating the disc. He adjusted the volume through the system to its maximum, reverberating between the walls of confined premises.

Picking up a simple chair standing against a wall, Edmund

hurried out of the hotel. He proceeded down the steps to the forecourt, where the dark, uneven cobblestones pressed through his slippers to his feet, past his red Porsche. Every step in that public street was another gesture of his independence from public view and discipline. In the centre of the street outside the lounge bar windows, he stood his chair.

Music filled his city home, in a streetscape concert where no concert had previously been held, for the only man to hear it. Edmund in his robe and slippers sat in the best seat in the house, drinking his Champagne. He sat quietly, as audiences did before orchestras.

The hotel and other buildings were the walls of a great concert hall, as if the street were built to be an auditorium. Chords resounded between buildings, drums beat through walls. Windows oscillated. Waves of soul rode through him, as his arms made motions to the tempo.

Feverishly he clapped after the pieces he most enjoyed. "More!" he shouted. "More!" Edmund finished clapping before his hands were sore.

Sitting there was his chance to feel the inspiration: the composer's mind and heart. Crowds at concerts corrupted the recitals, but no audience distorted the airs and concertos sweeping through the streets. Only he and the music playing for him were there, in the performance that he alone commanded.

The concert made the air already clean and fresh more so. His blind eyes closed to see only music, stirring in the waters of his mind. Slowed melodies made the world tranquil. Bolder melodies were majestic. Edmund hummed and murmured the sounds that he was almost learning, always listening to the music.

Music he could've heard at any time he heard sitting in the street, dressed as if he were in his lounge room late at night. Somebody hiding in a room behind a window might've been watching him, but nobody complained about the noise. Nobody sounded his car horn at the strange man obstructing his journey along the street. Only someone watching him would believe what he was doing; Edmund would later try to convince people who weren't there what he had done.

He might've looked more like a lunatic than a rebel to sit there as he did, but he couldn't be a rebel when no one remained against whom to rebel. The police and mental health professionals would've interviewed him doing what he was doing one week earlier, and then detained him if they believed he was dangerous to himself or other people. They wouldn't have been concerned about a person doing as he was doing in the garden of his home, perusing daffodils.

Nobody could see him and the city was his home, without public imposition. When the world was again as it had been, his friends and he would sit and stand in formalwear in that comfortable lounge bar, the women in sequin dresses off their shoulders, while waiters in dinner suits served them canapés and brought them aperitifs to drink and fresh oysters in their shells. They'd laugh bemused at what he'd done that day.

He'd imagined company, but he had no company. No friends or women beautiful were there, no waiters with canapés.

Were Candice in a seat beside him, Edmund might've held her tender hand or she might've placed her hand in his, feeling each other's skin, only pulling them apart to clap each piece fulfilled. If she let him, he would turn his head towards her and gently kiss her cheek, although she would've been embarrassed if anybody saw them. He might've glanced at her and she at him, before she looked ahead again.

An image of her waiting for him early Monday evening formed in Edmund's mind: her long black dress and shadowy lace adorning her while she reclined in a comfortable large chair in her apartment, reading a magazine of articles she would easily recall in later conversations. Her feet in stockings would've rested, with her tight, tall, black shining shoes beside them on the carpet. Soft powders and neat lines of colour sweetened her carefully prepared face, her blonde hair smooth with turns of style. Around her thin pale wrist was most likely her small dress watch. Tickets for two good seats at the concert hall might already have been in her elegantly unobtrusive handbag, with shining sparkles of black links hanging from its sides, ready for her to pick up from the table when Edmund pressed the communication button outside the building door. She might've contemplated Edmund ringing her from his office, suggesting they meet each other at the hall. Her only fur, a thin silver fox pelt given to her by a long-past boyfriend, might've hung across an armrest of the chair.

Edmund imagined her when he telephoned and said he would remain working at his office: tears gripping the corners of her eyes and smudging the colours she'd drawn there. If anyone dared try to impose an excess of work upon her, then she protested with aplomb and smiling tact reserved for people not her friends. If she seemed to be abrupt with people who could've been her next acquaintances, then it was because she was saving her time and energies for the people who could be her friends and lovers. The sentiments she'd tried so hard to infuse upon Edmund's working mind hadn't persuaded him to her philosophies. Talking about him with her friends had become better than trying to talk with him about priorities.

Had Edmund left his office to be with her that night, he might've heard the music live that he was hearing in mere recording. He'd have seen the faces of a philharmonic orchestra and enjoyed the companionship of an audience sharing the experience. He could've learnt what Candice learnt and gone with her wherever she had gone. He might've woken near her Tuesday morning, wherever she had slept, but if she'd woken as he woke that morning she wouldn't have done what he had done. She would've continued searching for people after he stopped. She wouldn't have sat alone as Edmund sat in a concert in the street.

He wanted her to understand him when he talked about the things he'd done those days, confiding in her his observations and listening to her confiding hers in him. Neither one of them needed to have said anything profound, although some among the words they spoke would've been memorable to know. They would've listened to each other, soon forgot much of what they heard, but been better for what they said and did together. She might've chastised him for having taken his new car and other loot. She might've rebuked him for letting the intruder leave without telling him what happened to their people. She might have felt the things he'd felt, validating them because she did.

The air had become cooler, and Edmund set his empty glass on the ground beside his chair, pulled his bathrobe tightly to him, and rubbed his hands together. A choir sung the passion, but once rousing sounds and throngs of triumph were strangely unaffecting.

He might've cared too little about his solitude in a city without people, or too rarely noticed that he cared, until his time alone had ceased exciting him. He wondered what that said of him and what it condemned in all of them. His time alone in a place for people was just a foolish chance to be a fool.

Edmund hadn't set the sound system to repeat playing the disc, and the orchestra finished its performance. He'd clapped enough not to need to clap the conductor and musician great performers any more. The air was silent.

Listening to the silence, Edmund heard the tiny squeaks, scrapings, and mutterings of birds breaking the thin air. Being there should've been more fun. Recorded sounds weren't human sounds. Bubbles in a bath weren't the sense of a loving woman's skin. The trappings of his life had become the life for which he'd yearned, but still Edmund found it wanting. It remained a failure for anybody longing to be touched. More than he'd understood two days earlier, he needed to hold her hand.

He'd heard enough that day. Edmund wouldn't attend another concert without someone at his side.

A cool breeze blowing between buildings blew at the tails of his long bathrobe, the air cold and brisk against his legs, carrying his chair back to the hotel. His other arm dangling by his side, his empty glass hung from his fingers, before falling to the lounge bar floor. The day was like any other, but had become so late that only he in his nonchalance remained. The waiters and waitresses were elsewhere.

Conversations to which he'd been a party and those he'd overheard uttered again within his head. They might all have stories to tell about those days, but for Edmund going nowhere and finding where he was.

13

THE POWER GONE

On a mahogany desk in Edmund's suite was a telephone. The small light that shone if someone had left a message remained dark.

Edmund prepared to pick up the telephone handset and dial the digit to access a telephone line external to the hotel and then the number to Candice's mobile telephone, but hesitated. She might hear the ringing telephone, see the numerical display identifying the incoming number without recognising it, and not answer. She might wait to hear who spoke before picking up her handset, while Edmund lost his mind in sweet pretence that she was speaking live to him. Edmund romanticised her heart behind that perfect voice: that captured memory from too many days ago.

Her recorded words and tones wouldn't change because of anything he said, but he would invite her to share the suite with him. If she invited him to her apartment then he would go.

If she didn't answer or reply, would he dial random numbers with scant regard for the time of night or day at places that he called? He wasn't longing for another stranger to be his next acquaintance but for the woman to be his lover.

Edmund picked up the handset, but only the constant tone

of something wrong came from the earpiece. He slapped the handset on the receiver.

He took his mobile telephone from his jacket pocket, but it could not find a network. "Damn!" he said aloud. "Damn."

If the fault lay in the exchanges, satellite connections, or thin towers atop buildings then other telephones fared no better. Candice wouldn't telephone him before their world of people trickled back to town. She mightn't speak to him afterwards.

The hum of heating, air conditioning, or other ventilation units he'd not previously noticed stalled, winding down. Edmund listened to the change, until the room that once subtly pulsed to the murmuring of power fell quiet.

The electronic display of the digital clock was dark. He flicked the switches on the wall for the sitting room lights and then the bathroom lights. They didn't shine.

Edmund examined his new watch as if too should have stopped, but he put it to his ear and heard it ticking. The time was nearing one o'clock.

The small refrigerator in the bar cabinet no longer rattled a small sound. He opened the door to where the air remained cool, but the small light didn't shine.

Outside his high window, the clouds had become greyer and more numerous since last he saw them, obstructing the sun and light. Lying in still life panorama, the lights no longer shining from the docile shelves of building storeys must once have been bright, for everything was dark without them. They left their blackest shadows on the floors of shops and offices. Every electric wire might once have buzzed with energy to lights, machines, and moving aids. The city circuitry had sounded noise he could no longer hear.

The cessation of the system might've given Edmund more or less to fear. A political leader or military commander might've decided to shut down the electricity, to subdue a city in which perhaps only one man remained. The decision-maker mightn't have known Edmund was still there, trapped in a high building, or might've known he was. The hotel lift could no longer carry him back to the streets, and the suite that had been his tower overlooking his domain, much higher than its storeys, had become his prison cell. The king in his great kingdom was the only prisoner there.

Some of the people he'd been content never to see were the people who could revive the electricity supply. His life depended upon the skills of people he never knew and about whom he'd rarely thought. Power would not return without the people.

Edmund raised his hands in fists of travesty above his head. His eyes closed as his arms and he fell slowly forward against the glass, imagining voices he'd heard too rarely through the passing of his years. Theirs had been lives when everything was everything, except the people in them. Edmund wanted to know the people they had been.

His thoughts slowed in the darkness in his head. He wondered who but he could hear them.

Edmund's eyes gradually opened, to see again the place in which he stood. Among the sky of clouds were two distant helicopters moving slowly across his view. Edmund began waving his arms, frantically calling at them through the window, but they continued traversing space away from him. "Here," he called out, but no one outside the glass could hear him. If a pilot noticed him then he would point up to the roof or down to the ground where they could meet, but the helicopters didn't change their course towards him. "I'm a human being!"

He pressed his face against the window to keep the helicopters from slipping out of sight, until he couldn't see them anymore. He studied all corners of his view, before a long sigh came from his chest. His breath left a patch of fog on the glass.

At least one door from every floor led to a mandatory long well of fire stairs down to the open air, through which guests and staff would flee if flames engulfed the building. They were Edmund's only means to leave.

Necessities were for thirst and hunger he would later feel, but Edmund couldn't know whether he'd need food and beverage to last hours, days, or weeks, and whether he'd consume them alone or among huddled hordes far from their private homes. If that afternoon he drove upon the people coming back to town, then his next meal might be in his apartment.

Most food and beverage in the suite was heavy. He could salvage nothing else if he carried them downstairs, on what would be his only journey down.

The open bottle of Champagne barely bubbled. Edmund poured the remaining liquid down the sink in the small kitchen of his suite, the rich aroma parting.

Water no longer poured from the taps. Edmund's unshaved whiskers from his cheeks and chin scratched his fingers. He couldn't wash his face clean without water, but bottled water was better left for drinking.

His right hand lightly brushed the crumbs from the sitting room table into his left, which dropped the remnants of his foodstuffs in a rubbish basket with the bottle. The last fish eggs in their jar might be preserved in the refrigerator. Cartons of milk were becoming sour, but didn't yet smell through their packaging.

Damp towels lay in the bathroom. The hotel bathrobe hung over a chair. The hotel slippers lay on the floor. When the civil emergency of whatever kind had passed, faceless stewards wearing nametags no one read would again push metal trolleys though hotel hallways, replenishing the items Edmund had consumed. Maids to whom guests smiled without conversing would change the linen and clean the room, keeping wasted items left behind.

Edmund's new coat, suit, and shoes weren't crafted to be comfortable walking down long scores of stairs, but wearing them was easier than carrying them in his arms. They could have been his gifts to the hotel, paying his tariff, but he dressed back into them. His telephone, wallet, old ring of keys, and the key to his new car were in his jacket pockets. He draped his new tie around his neck.

He'd become a pauper, clasping his disjointed possessions heavier than he'd expected them to be. His shopping bag, briefcase, and umbrella made the thief seem like a fool, but he could be nothing better in his predicament. The lord of crystal manor had become another vagabond in someone else's home.

Wearing his coat-covered suit, Edmund opened the door from his suite. A window at each end of the hallway accorded some light of day, as did the open door behind him. The porter's trolley on which Edmund had brought his new possessions to his brief home stood aimlessly beside the intransigent lift doors.

His possessions weighed heavily upon his open arms as Edmund trod along the hallway. Protruding from the wall above the fire escape door was a regulation green exit sign, which the law required to shine with battery power when the electricity had stopped but which was dark. A notice warned an alarm would sound if anybody opened the stairwell door; burglar alarms required battery protection so that thieves wouldn't cause a power failure or exploit one.

Edmund's load complicated his two hands, leaving only the few free fingers of his right hand to turn the door handle. The door opened, but nothing sounded. The hotel secure in its supplies had allowed the batteries to lapse.

Confronting him was deeper darkness. A spring mechanism overhead tried to pull the door shut again, in a precaution against fire, but Edmund's blind foot leant forward beneath his coat and held it open. Carefully he manoeuvred around it, until his back kept the door behind him open.

The dust of concrete walls and box surrounds hung against his face and nose. The safety stairwell was cold, with the pretence of a breeze when Edmund stirred the stale, dead air. The flight of steps and a steel railing upwards to the roof was useless. Those downwards in the dark faded into barely determinate outlines in the grey, deepening into black but for the stray light coming from the hall beside him. Edmund used his elbow to press a switch beside him on the wall, but the fluorescent lights affixed to ceilings above the stairs remained dark.

His leg and knee continued holding the door open behind him as he leant forward as far as he could lean, looking down the stairs ahead of him while he still had light to do so. The stairs paused and turned at a landing and a wall, before resuming their dreaded spiral into night. Nobody was coming there to lead him down the long journey in his blindness.

Clutching his possessions, Edmund stepped forward. He memorised the position of the first stair setting downward as the stairwell door closed behind him, but his memory faded as the last light behind him vanished and darkness swallowed him. A lock in the door behind him clicked.

Arching his back for balance and leaving his bag and briefcase on the floor beside him and umbrella in his other hand, Edmund's outstretched fingers of his hand searched the surface of the door for the handle that had been obvious a moment earlier. The cold handle held his hand, but the handle wouldn't turn inside the stairwell. Security was reason for it to open only for people entering the stairwell from the floors. The stairs and well around him were unwaveringly black.

The air was without motion, laden with the dust of aged walls and concrete ground, uncomfortable to breathe. Nothing might've changed and nobody might've been there for many years expired. Edmund might've been the first person to walk down those suffocating stairs burrowed through the middle of the building, carrying things that people fleeing a fire would've left behind. His only ameliorating grace was that Edmund didn't need to run.

His umbrella too unwieldy to be a walking cane or blind man's stick and his bag and briefcase back in his hands, Edmund scraped his feet across the floor so they would feel the void of the stair looming. He was strangely vulnerable in the abject blackness swept around him, as mere darkness didn't make him. His left arm touched the cold steel railing of the banister, which steadied his bulky body while his right foot groped carefully onward. His right foot found the edge of the first stair downward.

The sloping cold steel banister against Edmund's arm remained his guiding familiarity, as he carefully bent his left leg to creep down to the next stair getting lower. The unseen weight he carried in his hands dragged him down, while his body arched slightly backwards trying to balance. His feet and legs settled briefly on each stair, before his next leading foot crawled over each small precipice down to the next. The stairwell in a silence echoed with the scraping and his steps, incrementally inching downwards in the dark.

The stairs and world were much too dark to waver into grey.

The railing turned, the floor remained flat. He'd reached the first landing: a mark that he was making his long way.

Always moving slowly and with his arm against the railing, Edmund's feet scraped little steps in a semicircle on the floor. His eyes must have adjusted to the darkness, for a soft sliver almost of light appeared on the next landing below him, too weak to leave a shadow. The light beneath a door to a floor of empty rooms didn't illuminate the stairs ahead of him, but the sliver was a reference point towards which he worked, distinct from the darkness he despised. His feet reached the edge of the first stair of the next passage, paused, and proceeded further downwards.

Edmund was timid and ignorant, compelled to be cautious in the black as he grappled for the edge of each engrossing stair. He was a helpless blind man, a cripple, carrying his burden in his arms in a life once without cripples. He reached the next landing, where the door was no more likely to open to daylight and to refuge than was the door that first ushered and confined him. His arm against the railing, he stepped slowly around the landing and continued traversing downwards through the night.

The journey was more daunting for making it alone. Edmund thought of talking aloud, making one side of a conversation pretending somebody was with him, but he needed all his thoughts for finding his next steps trekking down. The thin sliver of light under the next door below him reminded him of the walls too close and far away. He concentrated on the feelings through the edges of his feet, searching for each stair.

The steep stairs were increasingly uncomfortable to descend. More onerous than walking or running, the managed muscles in his legs controlling him were suffering in his careful, cautious strain. The bag, briefcase, and umbrella hanging from his hands were cumbersome to carry, but if he left them on the stairs then he would lose them. His heavy coat was hot and his exercise made him perspire within the clothes against his skin. The air across his face was much too heavy to console him.

Edmund sought a sliver of grey shades of light to guide him forward, but none emanated from the next door of wall below him. No place in which he'd ever before been was as wholly black as was the stairwell down which he crept: darker than just a place without lights shining, for it had no gasps of chance for short relief. Doors he couldn't see or open denied him time to lose in loitering in the hallway light beyond them, before he soon would need again to muster his possessions and return to the darkness in the day. He couldn't switch on a light with him in the stairwell or wait for one to shine. Instead, he staggered slowly through every floor of blinded darkness.

His arms and hands hurt in their grip and poise too firm to ease, holding his bag, briefcase, and umbrella close to him. Edmund walked too slowly and too cautiously, but he'd carried his new possessions too far to abandon them so soon. He wondered if he should regret having stayed in a suite so high at that hotel and never did. The multitude of stairs behind him were his journey past and those downward his journey coming.

The hotel that failed to light a stairwell during a power failure might also have failed to ensure the lowest stairwell door opened to the street. If not, he would drop his baggage at that last closed door and roam his hands against every wall trying to find a door to open. If a door opened to any floor then he could sit and wonder what to do, at least knowing where he was with light and air to breathe; he might able to break a low lying window and leap down to the street. He might be trapped on the roof, waving his arms at the first sight of airborne craft or crawling to the building edge and peering down for help, before rain began to fall. Worse still, he might be trapped inside that tower of night and dust, unable to escape. He would crumble in his clothes and die lonely in the dark.

Edmund paused at one landing, where the slivers of grey edges of grey light were almost discernible, and stepped slowly forward towards the wall where he expected a door to be. His anxious fingers ahead of him touched a door or wall, where he slid his fingers until they touched a handle. The handle didn't turn. The stairs remained dark black.

He felt lost, for the first time in his life. He felt weak, and realised he must once have felt much stronger. He felt insignificant, having once presumed he was important. He felt timid, and must once have felt all-powerful. Only his office walls had hid him safe. The losses of his life risked revealing the person he'd always been, but he had nothing else about which to contemplate.

Perspiration cluttered the heavy clothes he wore, but Edmund resumed stepping slowly down, carrying his possessions. His muscles and limbs were sore, until finally he stepped onto a floor beside which wasn't a landing but a wall. The railing stopped, and left his arm. Ahead of him, at the end of an aisle of darkness, was a line of light thicker and brighter than the slivers of light he'd seen under other doors. A subtle trace of sound and breeze might've been coming with the sunlight from the street, beyond which might be space.

Edmund moved quickly along the corridor towards the little light, almost stumbling, before recovering. Trying to maintain a straight line, his arms in their coat sleeves ran along a dusty wall, until he stood close to the light. He worked his hand until it found and held and turned the handle of a door. Preparing his flinching eyes for the bright lights of day, he slowly pushed open the door. The scolding light and cooling air rushed around the door against him. His painful eyes squinted, blinking rapidly helping them adjust, while the rest of him revelled in relief.

The open doors admitted a tender breeze across his face and hands, refreshing his mouth and lungs breathing freely again. The realms of light doused him, still holding his bag, briefcase, and umbrella. The breeze implied a place from which it came and a place to which it headed: a freedom through which his slowly adjusting eyes could see and feel the clean air moving.

Edmund pulled the door wide open and stepped forward, allowing the fire door to close behind him. He dropped his bag, briefcase, and umbrella to the ground and shook his sore arms in the air, flexing muscles he didn't want to feel. He stretched his legs and ankles, slowly becoming well again. The clothes and underclothes that sweat had joined to his skin became loose again, and he ran his hand through his mangled hair to breath air onto his scalp.

The streets of the city were brighter than the stairs had been, but were drab aside what he remembered them being. They were quiet, as they were when last he walked upon them, but the city had died since then. The uppermost floors of the hotel were higher in the engulfing clouded sky than they'd ever before been. The silent city centre had never been emptier than it was empty to him then.

The quiet began to waver. From the silence stirred a familiar sound. Edmund turned towards the street and heard the mumbling of a vehicle, not knowing what to do if the yellow car returned. The intruder might be with his friends. The brandy glass warmer worth fighting to keep wasn't worth dying to retain, if the altercation or risk of one progressed so far. Nothing he could buy or sell was worth dying to possess.

Edmund's possessions remained his, but he would gladly give them to anyone who assured him he was safe. He started walking towards the noise becoming louder, trying to identify it. He started to run, as a military truck sped across an intersection ahead of him and quickly disappeared from view.

The panting of his lungs subsumed the declining sound of the engine and rushing wheels, until he reached the open street, looked where the truck had gone, and saw nothing. Turning around, the street from which it came was also empty. If he'd learned something of the day, then he dreaded what he knew.

14

VAGRANTS

Edmund dumped his possessions in the front passenger seat of his Porsche. Concrete and other dust and dirt had soiled the sleeves and sides of his once dark coat, but slapping it dirtied his hands without cleaning his coat. He dumped his coat on the car floor, so that was all it soiled.

Edmund started the engine, ready to leave, when the warning light shone from the fuel gauge on the dashboard. The car needed more petrol before he could drive too far, not knowing where he would sleep that night, but electricity powered petrol stations as it powered so much else. Edmund stopped the engine, slumped forward against the steering wheel, and contemplated his new predicament. The sports car travelled faster than he needed to go, but the tank of his abandoned old sedan, less powerful and flash, contained petrol, if no one had taken it. The key to his old car was with the other keys on his key ring.

No longer driving brazenly, Edmund drove the best car in which he would ever sit back to the broken showroom, slowly reversing it back through the open doors and parking it in the place where he first saw it. Small pieces of plate glass lay on the bonnet of his cumbersome sedan and on the ground around it, spilt there when he'd broken into the showroom. Carefully examining his car for marks and scratches, Edmund removed fragments of broken glass and dropped them in the gutter for society to sweep.

He carried his possessions from the sports car to his lacklustre, lesser car, moving his dusty coat from the floor of one car to the other. Returning to the office into which he'd broken, past the timber desk he'd crashed into the door, Edmund replaced the Porsche key on the cabinet hook from which he'd removed it.

The desk drawers were unlocked. The uppermost drawer contained pens, pencils, and other office stationery, but the second drawer contained a small, innocuous battery-powered torch, which salespeople sometimes used to inspect and show prospective customers the finest workings in the vehicle interiors. The showroom cars were worth more money than many people would earn throughout their lifetimes, carefully crafted by designers, engineers, and constructors as skilled and diligent as any on the earth, but all Edmund wanted was the torch.

Edmund picked up the black handle of the torch, pressed a button on it, and watched the beam of light shine across the room. He smiled, as he hadn't smiled for a while, leaving the car showroom without looking at the cars.

Sitting again in his dark green sedan, Edmund's business clothes and shoes stifled him, unlike the comfortable casual clothes and shoes into which he'd first dressed that morning. They were probably still in the department store, lying on a chair where strangers couldn't see them.

Edmund returned there, where obvious among the clean reflections along the department storefront was the broken glass and black curtain across one display window. On the ground were the fragments of shattered glass Edmund spilled when last he was there, among which the steel litterbin lay on its side. The litter he had dropped when he emptied the bin was scattered in a mess, whether from wind, birds, or dogs.

The air was cold when Edmund stepped onto the street, and he dressed back into his long coat warm to wear. Carrying his torch and bracing himself, Edmund pushed aside the curtain and climbed through the broken window, when the warmongering sirens of the store alarms shrieked again. Passing the mannequins, porcelain, and fallen little shoes, he clamoured back into the dark department store. He covered his bare ears with his hands, and hoped the noise didn't frighten anyone away.

The sirens eventually abated. The store was again quiet.

Unlike the darkness through which he'd descended from his distant hotel suite, that darkness ended when a single ray of light shone from his torch. The far end of the roaming beam glided across shapes and shapelessness, illuminating dead mannequins and dying displays etched into the dark, casting relentless shadows reaching nowhere. No more the rich proprietor, Edmund returned a thief in the night.

The store bright when last he saw it had become a mountain cave, almost frightening for his unadjusted eyes slowly adjusting back to night. The high ceiling gave way to a hollow space through which was the higher floors: a thick void into more abject darkness.

He could take everything he wanted, but he wanted little there. Among the produce in the stores, only food and beverage were still important: staple foods to keep without refrigeration and eat without cooking. Most foods that wouldn't rot were bland, and blocks of simple chocolate would be easier to carry and keep than the boxes of good confectionery in the store.

Edmund didn't need what once he thought he needed and knew only some of what he wanted. He was alone, master of everything he saw, and he saw that it was nothing.

Edmund's searching trail of light explored the floor in front of him in the motions of his steps. The sound of his leading shoe striking against the floor reverberated through the air and walls around him and he stopped, uneasy with the sound it made. He walked more gently, following the beam of light ahead of him, but still the little noises spread from his shoes into the shadows. The interior of the store would've been quieter than the streets, but for Edmund walking there.

Idle escalators were tall, steel stairs. The torchlight guided

Edmund and his hand sliding up the rubber handrail steadied him, climbing through the cavities of the store.

His old clothes were where he'd left them. Placing the torch on a counter to light him, Edmund removed his new jacket, tie, trousers, shirt, shoes, and socks, and dressed back into his casual clothes. Save only for his drab and dirty coat he needed in the cold, he left all the store's clothes on the chair, as someone trying them on without buying them would. His clothes and shoes at home would be enough, as they'd never before been.

A distant sound, like that of a bolt unlocking, came from the escalator well. Edmund turned towards it, to see a hint of light from what had been a black hole. He switched off his torch, when the light downstairs was unmistakable.

Edmund listened. He might have heard a footstep.

His little patch of torchlight in the night led him slowly back to the escalator well. Looking down from high, the ground floor was brightly lit, not with fluorescent lights from all directions but daylight from only one: the direction of the doors. The refracted light reflected on the sharp ridges of the escalator stairs, guiding his feet down. His torch became superfluous, while his hand held the rubber handrail heading down.

Stepping down the final escalator, the open entrance door and shutter appeared ahead of him. Outside was a rising wind Edmund hadn't heard upstairs. Inside, he looked around at light and shadows less daunting than they'd been. Reaching the ground floor, he continued to the open door until he noticed, against the curtain from the display window through which he'd come, the outline of a shape something like the solitary figure of a man, apparently accustomed to standing without motion and to rarely being noticed.

"I can't say I like what you've done with the window," said the stranger in the dark, his high-pitched voice like that of a playful, prepubescent child.

Edmund stopped. People returning to the city should've been streaming along streets in noisy cars, not lurking in empty stores where people waiting for them mightn't see that they were there. "Did you open the doors?"

"I used to work here."

Edmund shone his torch towards him. The bedraggled coat and other loosely fitting clothes that hung from him were those of a man Edmund would've called a homeless bum, without knowing anything about him. Dirt made patches of his grey coat black, on which dust left patches grey again. Dirt and dust had also soiled the coat that Edmund wore, but his at least was clean inside. The man was slightly slouched, but wasn't obviously malnourished or unwell. His crumpled brown felt hat couldn't cover his ragged, greying hair.

"Careful," said the man, when the torchlight neared his eyes, turning his head away.

A wiry grey beard concealed most of his face. Torn gloves covered his hands, hiding the worst of his long age. Edmund switched off his torch.

"Well," the man smiled, "either this store is both of ours or it's neither of ours."

"Should we be evacuating?" asked Edmund, approaching him.

"Why would we do that?"

Edmund couldn't answer him, but didn't feel foolish for having asked.

"Hello," said the figure suddenly, offering his gloved right hand for Edmund to take and shake.

"Hello." Edmund's hands moved from his side but baulked. The figure's glove was dirty.

"I have a name," he declared, behind his coat and other clothes. "I used to be Robsley Devereaux, when I worked all the time, but you can call me Bobby."

"I'm Edmund Neale, still Edmund, and I still work."

"What makes you think I don't work?" countered Bobby. His voice alternated between flurries of frivolity, manic energy, and lethargy. "How do you know I'm not the manager of this store but I dress down on my days off, or that I work in a boutique?"

"Why would you live like you do if you don't need to?"

"Sometimes it's nice just being a person," smiled Bobby. "I might sleep in a bed as good as yours and like the things you like, but not like them enough to give my life away for them. Nobody should work so hard while anyone is poor."

Edmund didn't know whether to believe him. Whether he did was unimportant.

"Maybe I should call you Eddy," suggested Bobby. "Eddy and Bobby – what do you think of that?"

Edmund tried to think of something to say. He didn't understand the conversation of which he was just a part.

"No," said Bobby, shaking his head. "Eddy and Bobby, it sounds stupid."

"What are you doing here?"

"I live here, Edmund," he replied, before correcting himself. "Not here," he said, pointing one hand into the department store, "but here." He pointed his other hand to the streets.

"Where is everyone?"

"You don't know?"

"No."

"Is that why you stayed, Edmund?"

"Do you know what happened?"

"I sort of know."

"Tell me what you...sort of know."

"You should say 'please'," Bobby corrected him.

"Please tell me what you know."

"You could ask me how I feel today, Edmund."

Edmund sighed, wondering whether he was wasting time with a man who might've been insane. "How do you feel today, Bobby?"

"Fine, Edmund, fine," he smiled. "Thank you for asking. How are you feeling today?"

"I want to know where everyone is."

"Everyone but you and me, you mean."

"Yes," said Edmund. "Yes."

"People were scared of something. They might've been scared of everything. They'll be back soon."

"How do you know?"

"Look outside," said Bobby, slowly sweeping his hand towards the open door, reintroducing Edmund to a sight he'd already seen. "Nothing happened, Edmund. People get scared of so many things, and they should be scared of some things, but not of all the things that scare them. Maybe they like being scared, but they don't get scared of some things that should scare them."

"Are more people here?"

"Of course, there are! There are thousands of people here: some like you, some like me. I like to walk alone a little while each day, thinking about things. I saw your car. I saw the broken window."

The presence of other people, perhaps people like him, comforted Edmund more than Bobby's presence did; the city never had been empty. "I want to go to where the people who left the city went," said Edmund.

"Maybe they like being where they are, doing what they're doing."

"I'm not trying to bring them back," Edmund explained. "I want to find someone."

"Most people are looking for someone."

"I'm looking for the woman I should've seen on Monday night, although she probably won't want to see me."

"I'm surprised nobody told you what was happening Monday night," said Bobby. "You're obviously not one of the people from whom we were told to keep everything secret."

"What people?" asked Edmund. "What secret?"

"The funny thing is that if most people had talked about secret messages the way they talked about them Monday night, they would've been locked away – for their protection, not ours."

"Nothing was on the television, or radio, or Internet. I couldn't reach anyone on the telephone."

"Maybe that was you, Edmund," said Bobby, as if in idle conversation. "Maybe nobody wanted to talk to you." He started to smile. "I shouldn't say that."

"I couldn't have been the only person not to hear about the evacuation, aside from those people you mentioned from whom it was deliberately kept secret."

"People left throughout the night. Others wandered the next morning lost in the streets, until somebody like me watching from a laneway checked I could warn them to leave. Some never left their homes, but I see them when they stand near the windows."

"I searched for people," said Edmund, "but the only people I found were an old woman who wouldn't tell me anything and a young man who would only sell me what he knew."

"Maybe the people who saw you thought you should be alone?"

The popping of distant gunshot suddenly peppered the air, quickly followed by a barrage of rapid shots and the thumps and bangs of exploding mortar in what might have been a battle or many battles. Stepping against the wall, momentarily paralysed with the question of which way to run, Edmund peered around the corner through the open door to the street. He saw no combatants, explosions, or battle damage, but closed doors and windows from other buildings could conceal firepower. If people had hidden from Edmund for two days, then they might still be hiding, but be prepared to kill him in their last ignominy. There could be danger in all directions. "We should hide," he told Bobby, rushing across the store floor into darkness.

The threat that had evicted the people from the city was climaxing in a secret little war; the tolling might become the ringing of their deaths. Bobby slowly followed him.

Edmund stood behind tall shelves, around which he peeked to watch the street. The commotion out of sight continued.

Bobby stood beside him. "I remember," he said. "We needed to keep the evacuation secret from the terrorists and their imam."

"What were they threatening to do?"

"I don't recall."

A bomb would kill them without them noticing their demise. The wind might carry poisonous gases towards them, choking them with time to feel their tortured deaths. Airborne viruses might kill them with short or long suffering. Edmund looked back at Bobby. "Why didn't you go?"

"Oh, Edmund," smiled Bobby. "I suppose I didn't believe what people said. If something happened, there are lanes, little lanes, like hives, most people never notice, much like they never notice people like me, where my friends and I can disappear in a moment and they can never find us. We know the lanes because we look for them, but you can't find anything for which you're not looking."

"We can hide from terrorists but not from terror," said Edmund. "We can't hide from bombs."

"I know that," insisted Bobby. "I'm not stupid. I only want to hide from the people who planted them and the people searching for them."

"I never saw anyone searching."

"They were here, dressed in protective clothes they knew couldn't protect them. Small complements of scared soldiers with detectors investigated what they called anomalies."

"If they're scared, we should be terrified."

Soldiers presumably, police perhaps, were trying to stop the people who would've murdered them. The purported assassins might've been willing to die, blasting their brains to hell with dreams of deep paradise, enmeshing victims they didn't know with those they did. If they were wired to die with their carnage, then their means to mass destruction might still be at their fingertips. Rather than sedating them, gas canisters might make them press their triggers. Terrorists at their deaths would find the strength to detonate whatever they'd threatened to ignite. Sane citizens had surreptitiously slipped away on Monday evening, while Edmund was at the office.

The store had become a cage. "We might be trapped," said Edmund. He glanced down at the torch in his hand, switched it on to see it worked, and switched it off again. "Aren't you worried?"

"I didn't die yesterday," said Bobby. "I'm unlikely to die today."

The battle sounds paused, but the momentary break ended with more sounds before Edmund could conclude anything about it. Soldiers and terrorists might've been choosing their targets or changing weapons. Edmund was a desk jockey who knew nothing important. The sounds resumed, without anything to see.

The sounds of battle again stopped. Edmund listened, waiting for them to resume, but the city remained silent. For several minutes he waited, before tentatively stepping the long way to the open door, ready to hide again if anyone appeared. He reached the open door, poked his head outside, and looked around. The street was empty, although ambulances ferrying dead and wounded might soon roll into sight. Edmund walked quickly from the store towards his car.

Bobby followed him. "Can I please come with you, Edmund?"

"I'll take you somewhere you'll be safe, but then you're on your own."

"Why?"

"I need to find her, and when I find her and if she will let me, I want to stay with her."

"Is she someone you love?"

"I won't know if I love her unless I spend time with her."

"Can I meet her?"

Edmund glanced at Bobby's clothes. "We need time, the two of us."

"You can be so pompous!" Bobby told him. "You think you're confident, we call people like you arrogant, but you're plain pompous!"

"What about you?" retorted Edmund. "You dress to be something you're not. You pretend to be poor." Edmund stared at him, deliberating about whether he wanted their conversation to be about him, Bobby, or both of them. "We must go."

"Here," said Bobby, stepping away from Edmund to a plant pot on the footpath. Edmund watched Bobby reach down, collect some soil in his gloves, and stand up. "Look, here," said Bobby, holding out his gloved hands for Edmund to see the soil as he walked towards him. Finally, Bobby stood before him, holding the soil near his face.

Edmund studied the soil, before looking back at Bobby. "I don't understand."

Bobby thrust up his hands and wiped the soil across Edmund's face. Edmund pulled away, dropping his torch.

"Why did you that?" The tips of Edmund's longest fingers felt the soil on his face.

Bobby dipped his head and chest, dropping his hat to the

ground, and ran headlong into Edmund, tackling both of them to the ground. They wrestled without fighting: Bobby rubbing his dirty gloves against Edmund and his clothes that the footpath threatened to tear. More shocked than fearful of being hurt, Edmund tried to push himself away without hurting either one of them. Rolling on the ground and as he tried to crawl away, the footpath grazed his coat. The sweat of melee soiled his clothes. Bobby suddenly pulled away from him and stood up.

"What's wrong with you?" asked Edmund, dishevelled and awry, panting as he sat upright on the ground.

"You needed to know you might be like me."

"I don't need to dress like you to be like you."

"No!" exclaimed Bobby, thrusting out his long pointing finger and the dirty glove covering it towards him. "You don't."

Edmund looked at him, trying to understand. Bobby started to smile, as Edmund picked himself up from the ground. He brushed his dirty hands over the worst of the mess on his coat and face, but couldn't make himself clean again. Shades of grey and brown blemished the once blue coat that had been beautiful that morning, concealing the clothes he wore below them. Edmund picked up his torch.

"There, look," said Bobby suddenly, stretching out his arm and pointing his gloved fingers along the street.

"What?" asked Edmund, stepping forward into the direction Bobby pointed, looking for anything that moved.

"There!" said Bobby. "There!"

"Where, where?" Edmund continued stepping forward, focussing his eyes upon distances down the street. "I can't see anything." He looked up the sides of building blocks shrinking into sky. "What is it?"

Bobby didn't answer.

Edmund turned around. Bobby had gone. "Bobby," he said. "Where are you?" Edmund stepped back to the department store entrance. "Bobby?" he called into the darkness. The far end of his torch beam searched among the shapes and shadows for a dust and dirty figure. "We have to leave."

15

APPREHENSION

The only sounds along the street outside the store were the wind and whistles of birds, until another sound slowly rose through them: soft rumblings coming from all directions. The sound wasn't from a battle, but might've been another made by the antagonists. His long, dirty coat hanging from him and his torch still in his hand, Edmund listened carefully, trying to assure himself the noise was there and trying to decipher it. The rumblings became louder as he listened.

Edmund looked along the street in one direction from which a sound might've come, but couldn't see a change of shadow to suggest what creature he could hear. The sound was like an engine, but not quite.

He turned and looked the other way, towards another place from which sounds might've come. Only the sounds were there, continuing to grow louder, whirring among the building blocks from every side as much as from any one.

Edmund stepped away from the footpath, kerb, and his car into the centre of the street, turning in all directions for the sound, welcoming it towards him. Anybody coming with such a noise was good, would be relief: the populace coming home because the city was secure. It might be conquering troops having defeated the invaders. It might be the fanfare of festivities for people they had saved. Vehicles and marching bands might be streaming in a celebratory ruckus.

A giant golden float with a royal crown and the wand of a fairy queen might be leading a parade. Sitting high on the throne might be Candice, with the sparkles on her cheeks glistening and her red lips shining warmly. A smile rose through Edmund's face, if only she would see him.

The sound became loudest, when suddenly a large grey spinning arc and black bulge with it appeared above him, drawing Edmund's head and neck upward. It stopped above him, hovering, targeted upon him. The screaming spinning circle and overwhelming military helicopter hypnotised him; the rhythmic rotating blades pulsating against the late-day sky. The craft was large enough to carry several people and perhaps small enough to land in the street, but it remained hovering in the air, watching him.

Edmund stared dumbstruck, like a squirrel caught in car headlights at night. The pilot stalked him, trapping him.

Snapping Edmund's concentration, a black wagon marked with military colours and insignia appeared from a side street. Turning towards him, it overpowered the noise of the helicopter, before stopping near him. The wagon engine remained running, while the passenger door snapped open and a young uniformed soldier leapt outside, pointing his pistol at Edmund.

No open barrel of a gun had ever before stared down at him and his meagre small eyes. The menacing black weapon could kill him in one instant of another man's life.

An older soldier remained at the wagon driver's seat. The helicopter continued hovering above them. The younger soldier's eyes glanced briefly at the torch in Edmund's hand, before walking close enough to Edmund's car to look through the side windows, without touching the car. He surveyed the open department store door, broken display window, and litterbin on the ground. "One unidentified white male," he reported to the soldier in the wagon. "No other suspects visible."

Edmund had never before heard himself so described. So the soldier would see he wasn't carrying any weapons, he began spreading his arms and hands wide from his grubby, crumpled coat.

"Don't move!" the soldier screamed.

Edmund no longer thought of doing anything else. He stood motionless, slowly mustering the courage to speak. "I'm not a terrorist," he whispered, trying not to reveal his fear.

The wagon driver took a radio microphone from the dashboard in his hand, but Edmund couldn't hear what he said or heard. Military officers only had jurisdiction over civilians in city streets in extraordinary circumstances, but those days were extraordinary. With a clean uniform and carrying just a pistol, the young soldier didn't appear to have come from battle. The older soldier finished his conversation, stopped the vehicle engine, and stepped outside. He removed his pistol from its holster on his waist and held it defensively.

"I don't know who you think I am," said Edmund.

"Keep your hands where we can see them," said the younger soldier. "Lay face down with your arms out on the ground."

Edmund's coat fell away from him as he crouched downwards. The street was rough against his dirty but tender office hands, still holding the torch. Edmund lay with his arms stretched out from his sides and the cold coarseness of the ground at his cheeks.

"Let go of the torch," the younger soldier ordered him.

Edmund released the torch from his hand. It rolled briefly before stopping.

A gun still pointed at him, the two soldiers walked near him, scrutinising him. The older soldier kicked the torch towards the kerb, before kneeling down and patting his hands along Edmund's coat sleeves. He frisked Edmund's arms, body, and legs, striking something in a pocket of his coat. "What's that?" he asked Edmund.

"My keys."

"Using only one hand, take them slowly out of your pocket."

Watched by the soldiers, Edmund lifted himself up. "Not too far," ordered the younger soldier.

Edmund's hand and fingers gingerly moved to his pocket. He removed his ring of keys.

"Drop them on the ground."

Edmund released the keys. They rattled as they settled on the street.

"Lie on your back."

Edmund obeyed, lying immobile face upward to the uniforms towering above him, becoming a little giddy, even queasy. Beyond them, the black helicopter hovered in the air.

His arms stretched helplessly away from him. The street scratched his scalp. The afternoon air made him cold, lying spreadeagled with the sides of his coat lying open around him, exposing his casual clothes. The older soldier patted Edmund's chest and stomach, searching. He checked the internal pockets and lining of Edmund's coat, before telling the soldier pointing his gun: "He's unarmed."

The older soldier looked upwards and waved his arm. The helicopter flew away.

"Shouldn't we be getting away from here?" asked Edmund. Talking was difficult with his back lying flat and his neck and throat stretched long.

"You weren't getting away when we arrived. What's your name?"

"Neale, Edmund Neale."

"Your full name?"

"Edmund Sterling Neale."

"Serling?"

"Sterling."

His name was just words. Edmund lay patiently on the ground, the gun of one tall soldier pointed at his sore head, while the older soldier returned to the wagon. Edmund heard only the description "white male approximately forty years of age" from the words he spoke into the radio microphone, before walking back. "An Edmund Sterling Neale owns the car," he told the younger soldier.

The soldiers looked down at Edmund. "Do you have photographic identification?"

"My wallet is in the car."

"Do you always leave your wallet in the car?"

"I didn't think anyone would be here."

"Get your identification."

"I'll need to stand up."

"Stand up."

A pistol remained pointed at his chest as Edmund collected himself, pulled himself upright, and sat on the street. Cautiously, he reached out and picked up his keys. He stood up and used his car key to unlock his car doors from a distance. He walked slowly towards the driver's door and opened it. He removed his wallet from the side compartment and offered it to the soldier not pointing a gun at him.

"You open it," the older soldier told him.

Edmund opened his wallet. He removed his driver licence and gave it to the soldier.

The older soldier compared Edmund's face in the photograph with the face of the man before him. The first was clean with neatly brushed hair. The second was dirty and unshaven, with ragged, unkempt hair. He studied them closely, while Edmund thought about his facial features that didn't depend upon his lifestyle: his eyes, nose, and cheeks. "It might be him," the soldier told the other.

"We better check."

The older soldier walked back to the wagon and again picked up the radio microphone. "We need someone who knows Edmund Sterling Neale."

Edmund faced the younger soldier remaining with him. "Shouldn't we evacuate the city?" Edmund asked again.

"Have you something to tell us?"

"No."

"The terrorists are dead. The bomb is defused."

"The bomb?"

A single distant shot sprung from the streets. Edmund looked around. The soldiers didn't flinch.

"Why are you here?" the younger soldier asked Edmund. "Are you sympathetic to the terrorists? Are you an idiot?"

Another black wagon sped through an intersection near them. Edmund turned and saw it disappearing beyond the corner of a building block, wondering if it was associated with the shot. There might suddenly be scores of soldiers and hovering helicopters, scouring the streets. The city was awash with military motion.

The soldier at the wagon replaced the radio microphone to the dashboard. He slipped Edmund's licence into his shirt pocket, before looking through the windows into Edmund's car. He opened the passenger-side front door, revealing the briefcase, umbrella, and shopping bag. "Is this yours?"

Edmund nodded.

"Take everything slowly out of the bag. Put it on the ground."

Edmund didn't know if the soldiers' power and authority extended to making those demands of him but didn't know that they did not, in the circumstances in which they stood. He reached into his car and the shopping bag, from which he removed a folded maroon scarf. With the younger soldier's gun ready to fire, the soldiers studied the scarf, as Edmund carefully rested it on the street.

"Where is everyone?" asked Edmund, as he removed another item.

"No-one is returning," said the older soldier, studying each item Edmund removed, "until the roadblocks come down."

"I didn't see any roadblocks."

"You didn't go far enough."

The soldiers watched Edmund performing his chore. "They're nice clothes," said the older soldier. "Did you buy them? Have you receipts?"

Edmund could've manipulated the truth or simply been truthful. A lie could make that moment easier, when the truth would imperil him to prosecution for theft without excuse. He could refuse to say anything, when the soldiers would treat him as having stolen everything they saw.

"Did you work for them? Did someone give them to you?"

"I have money," said Edmund. "I can pay for everything I took."

"You would say that."

"I need clothes," said Edmund, gently protesting the extent of his innocence.

"You don't need fashion."

The soldiers surveyed the items lying on the street. "It all seems harmless," said the younger soldier. "It's what I'd expect a vagrant to steal."

"A vagrant with a car," added the older soldier. "Vagrants can be greedy." He turned to Edmund and ordered him: "Show us the bag is empty."

Edmund removed the bag from his car. He held it upside down.

The older soldier looked into it. He checked the car. "Put everything back in the bag," he told Edmund. "We don't want any litter."

Edmund continued to comply. "You shut down all communications out of the city, didn't you?" he postulated, hoping the soldiers would correct any errors he made. "The emergency services telephone number was overwhelmed by people reporting anything they saw or heard and by people wanting information. Otherwise, telephones were transmitting calls but not accepting them, diverting them to answering services to which they denied people access, pretending no messages were there."

The soldiers remained silent.

"Roadblocks kept away anybody answering my broadcast," continued Edmund, repacking everything back into the bag. "People refusing to join an evacuation don't attend public concerts."

"Keep packing."

"What I don't understand, is how you failed to detect me for almost two days?"

"What makes you think no one detected you?" the older soldier asked him. "Satellites and other surveillance saw you every time you stepped outside. You're not important."

Edmund deliberated upon the soldier's words, before the younger soldier interrupted his thoughts. "Come along."

The shopping bag was again full, standing on the street. "I can return everything to the store," said Edmund.

"Do you think that will make you less of a looter?"

"Yes." Edmund' arms hung down for the sleeves of his coat to conceal the watch on his wrist. "I do."

The two soldiers again looked at each other. The gun pointed at Edmund seemed slowly to relax, slipping slightly with the younger soldier's grip. "We're not here to detain petty shoplifters," the older soldier told his comrade. "We need only report what we find."

The younger soldier turned to Edmund. "Take it back."

The older soldier examined the fine English umbrella on Edmund's car seat, taking in his fingers a small store label. "This too," he told Edmund.

Carrying the shopping bag and umbrella, Edmund trudged back into the store, weary of the exercise but unwilling to assert his impatience. Moving in slow unison behind him was the younger soldier and his gun. The younger soldier remained at the open door, while Edmund proceeded towards the closest counter.

Placing the bag and umbrella on the counter, Edmund noticed a figure in the shadows. The floors of the store and aisles of merchandise was a warren in which a man dressed in black and grey could hide more easily than he could let himself be found, but Bobby stood where Edmund saw him. Neither man said anything.

"And the watch," called out the soldier behind Edmund.

Edmund hesitated, wondering when he'd noticed it. The store would want it back anyway, if anyone there learnt he'd taken it. Edmund slowly raised his hands, removed the watch from his wrist, and placed it on the counter. Edmund retained his dirty coat; he wouldn't do anything more than the tasks the soldiers demanded of him. He walked back to the soldier and they returned to the footpath.

"Put back the garbage bin and garbage, too," the older soldier told Edmund. The soldiers were humiliating him, but they could've arrested him.

Edmund picked up the bin and replaced it to its stand. He delicately picked up each piece of refuse and replaced it in the bin, along with the largest cuts of glass.

"Should we check inside the briefcase?" the younger soldier asked the other.

"I hate briefcases." The soldier turned to Edmund. "Open it."

Edmund again complied. The soldiers stood beside him,

watching him turn the briefcase towards them, unfasten the latches, and open it. Inside was a small sterling silver ornament.

The soldiers didn't touch anything, as they leant forward to examine it more closely. "What's that?" asked the younger.

"A brandy glass warmer."

"What's a brandy glass warmer?"

"You put kerosene in it and light the cloth wick," explained Edmund. The warmer was clean and wick unsinged. "You place a brandy glass in the rim, where the flame will warm it."

The older soldier picked up the peculiar curiosity and examined it, turning it over, raising it and lowering it apparently feeling its weight. "It isn't a necessity of life, is it?" he told Edmund. "It isn't anything you need." He returned the warmer to the briefcase. "This is more than mere pilfering," he told Edmund, unfastening a pair of handcuffs from his belt. "You're under military arrest."

"The warmer's mine," declared Bobby, his voice authoritative.

Three startled men turned around, facing a bearded figure in a torn hat and coat, standing at the open store entranceway. The older soldier removed his gun from his holster and pointed it at him. "Who are you?" he asked.

Bobby straightened his back and raised his head high. "Robsley Devereaux," he replied.

"I know that name," the older soldier responded. "You used to be someone."

"I still am someone, someone with a wonderful brandy glass warmer. Can you not appreciate such art? I gave it to my friend to look after for me."

"We found stolen merchandise in his possession," said the younger soldier.

"Rubbish you have," said Bobby. "If I were Edmund, then I would step back in my car and leave you to find terrorists and criminals."

"We have found a criminal, maybe two," said the older soldier, asserting their authority. "We have the power to shoot, if we must."

"You won't shoot us," said Bobby. "You know full well this

man is one of us: like you and me. You're soldiers, not bullies. You defend and protect us, not harass us."

Edmund had never before heard such an appeal to oaths and honours, such kinship between strangers. The soldiers looked at each other as Edmund looked at them, before they turned back to face the stranger. Bobby had gone.

"Stay there," said the older soldier, as he ran to the store entranceway, pointing his gun forward. "Don't force us to find you, Devereaux?" he called into the darkness. "We can surround this building and will shortly be restoring the electricity. You can't escape."

Bobby did not reply. The store remained silent.

The soldier turned back to his comrade, titling his head to Edmund's torch on the street. "Throw me that torch," he said, affixing the handcuffs back to his belt.

The younger soldier continued pointing his gun at Edmund, while he picked up the torch. He threw it towards the older soldier.

The older soldier caught it deftly with one hand. The torch alight, he stepped into the store, hunting the shadows of night.

Edmund turned to the remaining soldier. "Stay where you are," said the soldier, firming his grip on his gun. Bobby had made Edmund and him accomplices.

Less conscious of the gun pointed at him than he had been, Edmund patiently watched the entranceway of the store, waiting for the impasse to resolve. A helicopter passed overhead.

The sides of Edmund's eyes gradually noticed a small movement at a low corner of a storefront window. Bobby was watching him, holding his index finger over his lips to tell him to remain quiet. Edmund discreetly nodded. Bobby waved the back of his hand to tell Edmund to scamper away, but Edmund tilted his head and directed his eyes to the soldier pointing a gun at him. Bobby shrugged his shoulders, before again disappearing.

The young soldier glanced back and forth between Edmund and the empty entranceway. "It's only a department store," said Edmund.

The soldier looked back at Edmund's car. "Give me the keys," he told Edmund, holding out his hand. Edmund obliged. "You stay where you are."

The young soldier stepped into the store entranceway. "Are you there, Sergeant?" he called into the darkness. Edmund heard no reply. The soldier joined the thumb and first two fingers of his left hand and tapped his forehead, chest, and each of his shoulders in the sign of the Cross. He looked back at Edmund watching him, before looking again into the store.

The welfare of his comrade was surely more important, thought Edmund, than detaining the suspect of a crime no one committed. Edmund tried to will him to proceed into the store, out of Edmund's line of sight. The nearest corner was close enough for Edmund to reach and keep running until he found the burrows Bobby mentioned.

If Edmund fled from the soldiers then he would always be a fugitive, hiding in city holes as Bobby did. He would only see Candice by sneaking secret meetings with her in the darkest hours of night, if she were willing to compromise her life by seeing him. His only chance to be with her again, properly to be with her, would be for the military to release him to his recognisance or hers.

He wouldn't run away. Candice might be returning to the city; he would wait for her at her apartment.

The soldier remained standing at the entranceway of the store. Edmund remained standing by his car. Lying on the car seat was his open briefcase. The brandy glass warmer had been the impetus for the soldiers to arrest him, but when they returned, they mightn't think anything more about it. Edmund stared at the soldier who would shortly glance at him again, while his right hand edged towards the case he couldn't see. He surreptitiously took hold of the smooth silver, grasping it in his fingers. He brought it from the briefcase to his side, and slipped it into a large pocket of his coat. Reaching back into the car, he closed the briefcase lid.

The younger soldier turned suddenly and walked back towards Edmund. "Put out your hands," he ordered him, as he drew the handcuffs from his belt.

"What about my car?" asked Edmund, as the soldier snapped a pair of cold steel handcuffs to his wrists.

"We're impounding it until we know who you are," replied the soldier, closing Edmund's car doors. "The store owners can decide whether to prosecute you for stealing."

From the store appeared Bobby with his hands handcuffed together in front of him. Beside him came the older soldier. "What's your full name?" he asked Bobby.

Bobby's voice was muted. "Robsley Parker Devereaux."

"Have you any identification?" Bobby shook his head. "Have you an address?" Bobby shook his head.

The younger soldier opened the rear door of the wagon, into which the soldiers bundled Bobby and Edmund. He then closed it and bolted it fast.

16

PRISONERS

The military wagon remained stationary. Along the sides of the rear section were two metal benches for combatants, criminals, and other prisoners. A single light from the ceiling illuminated Edmund and Bobby. Subdued in their confinement, they sat with their heads bowed and shackled wrists resting on their laps, facing each other. Edmund's shoulder muscles were sore and tender, unsuited to slouching with his arms shackled together. A small, soundproof window of toughened glass separated their compartment from the soldiers sitting in the front section. A small rear grille let the prisoners see a little of outside.

Edmund stared, trying to comprehend what had happened to the kingdom and the king. Everything he'd collected that day was no longer his, but for the misshapen coat he wore and a nonsensical brandy glass warmer in his pocket. The perspiration of strains and scuffles soiled his body flesh beneath his clothes. His whiskered face and hurting hands were dirty if not stained. His hair was rough and ragged: the random turmoil of someone too poor or weak to care. The day began with everything to rule, but before sundown, he'd lost and found two sides of nothingness.

The conversations he recalled in hotel bars hadn't all been whimsical. "Did you see the riots in Los Angeles?" somebody asked. Patrons recited the news they watched on television as if they'd been witnesses. "The governor called in the military to shoot the looters after they started smashing stores." Wherever those people were since Monday night, they talked about the vacant city they'd left behind. He knew what he'd become.

"The city was about to be destroyed and all the people in it murdered," said Edmund, the sorrow in his eyes, "when everyone warned everyone to leave, but nobody thought enough about me to try to save my life. Was I not better than that, that no man or woman was sufficiently my friend to want to warn me?"

"Who would you have warned?" asked Bobby.

Edmund studied the stranger's face: the eyes beneath a grubby hat and above such grubby clothes. "You have become wise very suddenly," he said.

Bobby grinned. His eyes flashed, before they rested again.

"I would've called the woman whose photograph was on my office desk," said Edmund.

"She mightn't have wanted to be a mere photograph."

If Candice abandoned Edmund Monday night, however many days ago that was, he'd abandoned himself long beforehand. "I would've called a colleague I knew was alone at the office."

"Really?"

"The people we'd save aren't always the people who'd save us, anyway." The skin close to Edmund's right eye itched. His right hand dragged up his left hand cuffed with it for him to scratch his face, before both hands and cuffs slid back to his lap. "Why do you think the terrorists never detonated their bomb?"

"They might've lost interest in dying when they realised they couldn't kill enough of us."

People who'd never before met and people who'd seen each other much too rarely had shared their recent days outside the confines of their lives, with the only matters upon which to deliberate being life, love, and death. "If all they wanted was to disrupt us," said Edmund, "then maybe their deed wasn't bad."

The two men sat quietly again, constrained by their cuffs. The two soldiers remained in their compartment, looking along the street ahead of them and sometimes in their rear-vision and side mirrors. The soldiers' mouths moved in conversation between themselves. Edmund couldn't hear them, although a hidden microphone might allow them to hear Edmund and Bobby speaking.

Outside, through the late afternoon light, the sun slipped behind buildings, their shadows becoming longer on the streets. The afternoon was fading before the sun had set, shaded from the weakening light by buildings no longer casting lights of their own. Edmund had never realised the extent to which those lights lit city streets until they no longer did.

"Bobby," said Edmund, looking back towards him. "Did you mean what you said about me being your friend?"

Bobby smiled. He winked a shimmering eye.

"Did you mean what you said about the brandy glass warmer: that you thought it was wonderful?"

"You liked that watch, didn't you?"

Edmund muttered a small laugh. "I suppose I did."

Bobby slipped his hand into a pocket of his coat. He pulled out, just enough for Edmund to see, the wristwatch.

Edmund smiled, more at Bobby than the watch. "I don't need to own it to enjoy it."

Bobby slipped the watch back in his pocket. "Later," he said.

Other headlights passed them, but one set coming from behind slowed and stopped beside the wagon in which Edmund and Bobby sat. Edmund reached up to look through the front window, seeing the soldiers in the front compartment lower their side window and speak words Edmund couldn't hear to whomever was in the second vehicle. The second vehicle proceeded forward until it stopped beside Edmund's car, where a soldier stepped outside, carrying a round yellow clamp. The soldier crouched down and affixed the clamp, with equidistant claws, around a rear wheel of Edmund's car.

The wagon carting Edmund and Bobby started moving away, leaving the second vehicle and soldiers in sentry. "Relax, Edmund," grinned Bobby. "Take a few days away from work."

Edmund didn't understand the bedraggled man before him. Bobby's hat was decrepit, but his clean hair merely unkempt. His gloves were torn but Edmund hadn't seen his hands. "How did Robsley Devereaux become Bobby?" he asked.

Bobby chuckled. He leant back on the wall of the wagon, turned his face to the side, and closed his eyes. He settled, almost sleeping. "You only want to hear the short story."

"Give me the long one later."

Bobby's closed eyes squinted and blinked, without opening. His rows of teeth ground together. "I was the wrong side of forty without knowing the right side," he said. "Sitting at my desk in my comfortably big office, reading a report about the cost of paper clips pilfered by employees – paper clips, mind you, in a corporation that spent more money on caterers in a minute than stationery in a year – I realised all of us were wasting our time.

"If I had a wife then I'd have retired with her to a cabin in a forest, but my only friends were names on neat office doors. My only family were photographs on other people's desks. The only people with whom I could sit without caring about paper clips were the people cuddling sheets of cardboard in the park. There, I was Bobby, without pretence, drinking lukewarm, sugar-laden coffee and talking about people we'd met. A rich man whispers and buildings shake, but a poor man screams and nobody listens. The more time I spent with them, the easier not spending time anywhere else became. I know I'm getting old, but having too little time and spending it wisely is better than having too much and wasting it."

Edmund waited until he knew Bobby had finished reciting his reflections on the past. "I was greedier and more ambitious than I admitted," said Edmund, "boasting my diligence and courting favour from people feigning work without anything worthwhile to do, but not Candice. She worked to earn money to do other things, to buy food, shelter, and a few toys with which to play, while she developed a wealth of friends she said made her richer than was anyone without them. Nothing tapered the time she shared with people for whom she cared."

"Mind you," grinned Bobby, opening his wide and frivolous eyes, straightening his head, and looking towards Edmund. "That's my version of events."

"What other version is there?"

"A newspaper journalist wrote that I cracked, broke down, unable to cope. He was probably right."

A wry smile crept through Edmund's face, strangely satisfied to have seized a chance that lasted a short time and wouldn't come his way again. "A journalist might write the same thing about me," he said, "but I was a sane man in an insane situation."

Bobby sat upright, startling Edmund. "That's right!" he exclaimed. "So am I!"

Edmund started to laugh. Bobby laughed with him. Their stains and soils were much alike, but if they made Edmund seem crazy they made Bobby seem not. The amenities of Edmund's life would again be those they'd been two days earlier: amenities without utilities. If Candice would be with him again then he wouldn't regret his brief adventure, but if she refused then he would regret Monday night. The journey back would be easier and more difficult than the journey out had been.

The falling night outside suddenly became bright. Edmund sat quickly upright to see all he could see through the front window of the compartment. Across the road ahead of them was a long barricade, with soldiers and civilian police patrolling. Beyond it was a crowd of people Edmund couldn't measure, some watching the military wagon approach, slow, and stop at the side of the road.

The older soldier driving the wagon made another radio conversation Edmund couldn't hear, while the younger soldier stepped outside. Outside the wagon rear door, the bolt that sealed Edmund's and Bobby's small prison released. The door opened. "Out you come," the younger soldier told them.

Edmund, facing Bobby, tilted his head towards the open door and air. Bobby stood up and stepped surefooted out onto the street. Edmund heard the gasps from the crowd. He, another ragged man in a dirty coat and handcuffs, stepped out, but the handcuffs binding his wrists and arms disturbed his balance and he stumbled to the road. Somebody screamed. Bobby helped Edmund drag himself up, when Edmund turned to face the crowd. A mother held her young child close to her side. Among the mobile telephones pointed at him and Bobby, filming them, were several large news cameras.

"Wait here," the soldier told Bobby and Edmund.

The street lights that accentuated the shadows from Bobby's beard and hat surely did the same to the dirt on Edmund's unshaven face, while the cuffs on their wrists dragged down their necks and shoulders. The two men stood conspicuously close to the wagon, waiting helplessly to be led, while the apprehensive glares from a hundred strangers under lights beat down upon them: two dishevelled effigies in grey, herded before the mob.

"Why are we here?" Edmund asked the young soldier.

The soldier didn't answer, while spectators in the crowd whispered to each other. Edmund thought he recognised the tall man with ginger-coloured hair staring at him, until the man realised Edmund was studying him and turned away. A police officer turned towards the man, who shook his head. If he was someone Edmund met in his good suits without noticing, then Edmund preferred that no one recognised the figure he'd become. Edmund still hid beneath the face and clothes he wore.

"Please move to the side," a policeman told the people across the barricade, as police pushed aside the crowd. Through the passage came a civilian police car, until it stopped at the far side of the barricade. The car doors opened, and stepping outside from a rear passenger seat was a young blonde woman whose face the street lights brightened in the night. Some cameras turned towards her, but their sudden lights made her flinch. Her deep red jumper and long brighter red woollen dress were the unaffected casual clothes she often wore.

Edmund was the handcuffed ruffian. She remained the figure cast resplendent beyond the barricade. "Candice," he called out, starting towards her.

Someone gasped. Candice stepped backwards, as did the frightened crowd in a tortured wake around her. Her policemen and women escorts stood close beside her. "Be careful everyone," a policeman said.

"Stay where you are," the young soldier commanded Edmund.

"What is this?" cried Edmund, lunging forward.

"We'll shoot you if we must."

Edmund tried to stop moving, but his wrists manacled together unbalanced him. He stumbled to the ground.

"You can tell them I'm not a criminal," pleaded Edmund.

"Stay where you are," the soldier again told him.

People and cameras focused upon Candice. With the officers beside her and soldier's guns protecting her, she looked quizzically down at the crude character in dirt barely kneeling on the road. Dust and mud speckled his unshaven cheeks and chin, his mangled hair, and the rubbishy coat hanging from his arms and body. Edmund knew she'd never before seen him as grubby as was the man crouched low before her. His bound wrists and arms were crammed between his chest and forward twisted leg. She surely had pity on him, but she didn't seem to know him.

If Candice knew the humbled man in rags was Edmund then she was slow to share that knowledge. He felt he needed to persuade her of his identity, to say something she would know that only he would say. "I'm sorry about the concert," he said meekly. "I should've gone with you, I know I should." Her eyes and face continued watching him. "I know what you're thinking," he resumed, gently mocking himself. "I'm always sorry, aren't I?"

She could've taunted him much longer, but she turned towards the older soldier. "That's Edmund Neale," she told him, and started back into the police car.

"Why didn't you warn me?" Edmund called out, kneeling on the ground without thought of standing up.

She turned back to him. "Didn't the people you work with warn you?"

"They didn't care."

"I'm sorry," she said. "I should've warned you."

"Thank God, you're here now."

She turned back to the police car beside her.

"Candice, wait," called Edmund.

She stopped, facing away from him, while he remained on the ground. "I attended a concert today," he told her, "with music by

Bach, but I grew bored without you. They were sounds, and all I wanted was to hold your hand in mine."

Candice slowly turned her head to one side for Edmund to hear her voice. "Would you rather touch a human hand than a computer keyboard or Dictaphone?"

"Your human hand."

"What will happen when next Hugh Garrett snaps his fingers, or waves pieces of silver before you? Will you release my hand from yours to go to him?"

"I'll tell him I have a commitment."

"What will you say when he says you have a commitment to him and your job?"

"I'll say that commitment is subject to my commitment to people I love."

She turned around. A smile slipped from his mind into his face.

"I got everything I thought I wanted," Edmund told her, "but I don't want it. The gold that glistened when I pursued it proved to be a pebble in my hands."

The older soldier ended his radio conversation. "The emergency is over," he told the police, without sense of station or status. "The barricades can come down."

The crowd began clapping and cheering. Some people climbed over and some crawled under the barricade, which the police officers began dismantling, clearing the road. Electricity flickered alight, as people held up their mobile telephones, presumably displaying the numbers of messages recorded during the previous two days, if telephone exchanges and computer servers had resumed their passages of communication and information. Transmitters presumably resumed broadcasting radio and television signals.

A last section of the reducing barricade separated Candice and Edmund still kneeling on the ground, unable to stand up. He looked up at the young soldier who'd restrained him, holding out his handcuffed wrists. "Please?"

The younger soldier turned towards the older soldier, who nodded. The younger soldier stepped forward, crouched down, and unlocked the cuffs from Edmund's wrist.

"Civilian police can deal with the crimes you committed," said the older soldier. "There's a lot."

Edmund stood up as a police officer carried away the section of barricade between him and Candice. He stepped forward as she did, the vagabond in a dirty coat and the lady in a clean dress. They embraced and kissed, unperturbed by the clothes they wore, the passion from his lips on hers pressed dust and dirt from his whiskers against her face. The substance of her strong body through too many layers of clothes between them was richer and more glorious than any other treasure he had held, softly malleable as he became gladly malleable with her. She kissed him as he kissed her, the love of her warm tongue enveloping his, feeling senses in his mind he'd never before sensed. The beating hearts Edmund felt in their embrace could've been hers or his.

Slow to leave Candice's lips, they slowly stepped apart, continuing their embrace. Some dirt from him was on her cheek, but she was no less beautiful for it. Edmund pulled his arm from her side and slowly raised his hand close to her face. With the soft side of his index finger, perhaps the only clean skin on his hands, he wiped away a small trace of dirt from her. "You need a bath," he told her.

She smiled. "We both do." She reached up her hand to brush the worst of his ruffled hair, before looking again at the rest of him. "You also need a new coat."

"This is my new coat." Some dust had soiled her lovely jumper and dress, and he stepped back to protect them from the dirt. She saw what he was doing and stepped closer to him again.

"She might want to kiss me, too," said Bobby, drawing Edmund's attention to him. Bobby lifted his handcuffed wrists.

"You never know," said the older soldier, who slipped his fingers into a pocket of his uniform and removed a key. He released the cuffs from Bobby's wrists. "Do you want someone to take you back to where we found you?"

"Not until they finish," replied Bobby, "if they finish."

The older soldier removed Edmund's driver licence from his pocket and returned it to him. The younger soldier returned to

Edmund his keys. "I'll arrange the release of your car, when we get you back there."

The crowds were dispersing along the footpaths, while fleets of buses filled with people streamed along the far side of the road to the brightly lit city centre. Edmund pictured trains banked up on railway lines in towns and other cities preparing to return more people to the precincts of their homes. Among the returning cars Edmund noticed a bright white taxi slowing as it neared them, with a small crucifix hanging from the rear-vision mirror. The driver smiled, before continuing his journey.

One of Edmund's coat pockets hung open. Checking the soldiers weren't watching him, Edmund put his hand into that pocket and removed a sterling silver ornament. It shone when everything else about him was drab. "I have a present for you," he told Candice, as he tendered it to her.

"What's that?" she laughed.

"A brandy glass warmer."

She laughed again. "What would I want with a brandy glass warmer?"

"Don't you like it?"

"Where did you get it?"

"I'll tell you later."

She looked at the ornament in his hands and at him. "It's beautiful, but it's simply an object."

He looked again at the shining silver, admiring but only admiring it. "Nobody on his deathbed wishes he had more money in a bank account or trophies on a wall," he said, before turning away. "Hey, Bobby!"

"Yes, Edmund."

"Have this." Edmund threw the warmer towards Bobby, who caught it in his gloved hands, nearly dropped it, but held onto it. "Look after it Bobby, and if you ever don't want it any more, then you better return it to that store."

"Thanks, Edmund," grinned Bobby, examining the warmer.

Edmund looked back at his dusty coat. "I better pay for this," he told Candice.

She smiled; her shining eyes. Her arms slipped inside his coat and around him. He held her closer, keeping them together.

ABOUT THE AUTHOR

Simon Lennon has lived, worked, and travelled throughout Europe, America, Australasia, Asia, and the South Pacific. He is married with six children. He is the author of the following books.

Fiction
The King of a Vacant City

Non-Fiction
Western Individualism
The End of Natural Selection
The Need for Nations
People's Identity
Of Whom We're Born
Biological Us
A Land to Belong
The Failure of Multiculturalism
Reclaiming Western Cultures
Christendom Lost
Aiding Islam